# Golden Years

ALI ESKANDARIAN

FABER & FABER

First published in 2016
by Faber & Faber Limited
Bloomsbury House, 74–77 Great Russell Street
London WC1B 3DA

This paperback edition published in 2017

Typeset by Faber & Faber Ltd
Printed in the UK by CPI Group (UK) Ltd, Croydon, CR0 4YY



A CIP record for this book
is available from the British Library

ISBN 978–0–571–32107–0

2 4 6 8 10 9 7 5 3 1

# Editor's Note

Editing is an act of communion. Most commonly, though not exclusively, this takes the form of a conversation – on the page, in the office, or in the pub – between author and editor. The creator of the fictional landscape meets the facilitator tasked with improving and finessing the book. There are disagreements. Then there are compromises. An editor should be ready to concede when there are moments of authorial intransigence. An author should stand firm when suggestions are made which compromise the integrity of his characters or the very moral compass of the novel.

The job of work that being Ali's editor involved never put me in this situation. There was no red wine, drunk from a shared bottle, spilled on the early drafts of the manuscript. We never got to celebrate that feeling of satisfaction on completion. And, of course, he will never see how I reshaped, tightened, and cut his raw, visionary prose. What Ali left us following his tragic death in November 2013, aged just thirty-five, was the first draft of a book teeming with life, love, sex, and the ambitions of eternal youth. And *Golden Years* took shape on the page and in my mind as an act of communion with a man gone from this world, who I would only know through the essence of his book and his music, and the mark he left upon those around him who loved his vaunting spirit.

So the novel you are holding is an act of love in the name and tradition of all editorial relationships on the furthest frontiers of literature. I hope Ali would have agreed to the 'improvements' – as I have to immodestly view them – to the structure of the book, which in Ali's draft was even more freewheelin' than in the version we have here. The prose itself I have mostly left as Ali wrote it. Sentences are the DNA of a novel, and from reading the first draft of *Golden Years* Ali's gifts for the form were clear. This love of language and its rhythms and his ability to capture the musical chaos of life represent the essential integrity at the heart of the book. My editorial interventions were conducted in an echo chamber but at each moment I tried to imagine what our conversation might have sounded like, and how he might have responded, had he lived to participate in that process.

Lee Brackstone

# GOLDEN YEARS

Their plane landed around six in the evening and it took a few hours for them to reach our apartment, but by then the new arrivals already had the look of free men.

'How about a beer, gentlemen?' I asked in Farsi after helping with their luggage. They sat around the kitchen table while I grabbed a few cold ones out of the refrigerator.

'Your first beers in America!' I shouted.

We drank a couple then smoked a joint before they relaxed enough to talk. I remember like it was yesterday the shell-shock of arriving in the States all those years ago. Our new friends were here now and not returning to Iran, we'd make sure of that. These guys, like a few before them, had risked their lives for their art by coming here.

'You came to the right place,' Koli assured them. 'Now let's have some fun.'

We took them on a short walk around our neighborhood in Brooklyn, talking all the while about their trip. The night was warm and breezy. The streets were alive with people. Their escape had not been an easy one, from what I was able to gather. The guys had been thrown in jail then released in time to leave.

'That's good . . . jail is good. Makes it easier for your asylum case,' I said as we walked into a bar.

# Brooklyn

Sometimes the answers come while you're standing at the mouth of a great canyon; other times the catalyst could be the smell of a cab driver's cheap cologne while he squawks away about Mohammed and his prophecies. They never want to talk about his forty wives or why we should believe God came to him through an intermediary in a cave and handed him the Old Testament plus the bible and said, 'Here you go, sonny, now it's your turn, go get 'em!'

Allison was born in a volcano on Easter Island. It was a Saturday and everyone was out statue-watching. She's an Aries like my dear Maman. It's Sunday and Allison is cooking our favorite breakfast: sautéed kale with garlic, onion, and mushrooms. Also grits with butter and fresh jalapeños, veggie sausage links and sliced wholegrain French sourdough.

Our new apartment smells like a home. The sun is shining through the wooden blinds and the window-unit AC is blowing cold. Duke Ellington's on the radio. I feel like a whole man. It's my second day of sobriety and this time I'm quitting for good.

'I love you, baby,' she says to me smiling, her blue eyes radiant and fully alive. The ground shakes and rattles as the express train plows up or down 4th Avenue. I slide over to where she's standing by the stove and grab her waist from behind, pull her close to me, and kiss her on the neck. She moans with delight and melts into me for a moment while turning the heat down on the kale. I move my hands down and squeeze her ass with intent. She's stirring the grits. Her short shorts are exposing her long smooth legs. I want to lay her down on the wooden kitchen floor and examine her from head to toe but my hunger gets the better of me. We're happy today, have been for a couple of weeks. Before that we had a couple of miserable weeks with no sex, no love-making at all. I was mostly getting drunk after work so by the time she got home from the restaurant late at night I was done for. When the loving is good it's the best.

When we met we were both lurking in the dark corners of the night, swimming in the frigid waters of single life in New York City. I fell for her the moment she walked in the door with a roommate of mine and a bunch of other people. It turned into a party pretty quickly. I had to have her but needed to be careful. You don't take a girl away from a friend without a little bit of tact and skillful maneuvering. We were both coked up within an hour of that first meeting and working on getting drunk. She played all the right songs, just sat down and asked if she could take over the music.

'Do you know who this is?' she asked me slyly.

'Sure, it's the 13th Floor Elevators. Great choice,' I answered.

'What do you want to hear?'

'Whatever you say.'

We shared a cigarette, passed it back and forth like we'd known one another for years. Stayed up until way after dawn. Then she left with my friend and I had to wait a while to see her again.

Every visitor was impressed by the loft I was living in back then, not that I was living there alone, or that a bunch of people living in a loft in Brooklyn is a rare thing, but this was a special place. To begin with it was in a very desirable location in Williamsburg, Brooklyn. I had tried to stay far away from Williamsburg but after a brief period of exile in Texas found my only real option to be living here with half-a-dozen other people, and many more coming and going at all hours. The loft was in the only old building standing in that part of the neighborhood. Amongst the dead shiny architecture it stood, defiantly, like a mountain before the flood.

There were four flights of stairs to walk up. On the fourth floor a heavy iron gate opened onto a long corridor with six separate loft apartments on opposite ends, some larger than others, but all large enough to house more than four at a time. Ours was the largest one of all. The views were spectacular from the windows alone but through the bathroom window one could access a rooftop the size of a football field which not only had unobstructed panoramic views of the city but a fifty-foot-high water tower and an eighty-foot chimney stack, both of which were visible from Manhattan if one wanted to find them. The plumbing was shoddy at best, the hot water never hot. If you wanted to make coffee on the stove you'd see a mouse jump from one burner to the other. If you turned on the toaster the whole building might lose power, and often did. When the upstairs neighbors walked around dust would fall upon us like snow. There was no real way to keep the place clean. The minute I walked in I knew I had to live there for a while and get my life back in order. It was a terrific hideout and I was a fugitive of sorts, in need of a fresh start. No address, no telephone, no connection to the people of the past, and I hardly knew any of my roommates, who were all recent arrivals from Iran, rock musicians who'd made it out. They knew me too, had seen me on Voice of America TV back in Tehran, which is illegally picked up via satellite. All these guys were much younger than me but that was no problem, I didn't feel old. I felt more alive than ever and in the next year we would enjoy countless wild times together. They gave me a couch to sleep on. It was the middle of summer and hot. I owned three T-shirts, two pairs of jeans, three pairs of socks, and my trusty black leather boots. Had almost no money and no job offers. I was a happy man. These kids were good to me and in time I'd be able to repay them for their kindness. The first order of business was to go on a two-month tour around the country with them as an opening act. I would get thirteen dollars a day to live on, a meager per diem no matter how you look at it.

The previous year during my self-imposed exile from New York I'd gone through a transformation of sorts. I was no longer whole or holy, had been forced to scrounge and scratch around. My music career and relationship with my long-term girlfriend had come to a fiery and sudden end and I'd found myself back in Dallas, living with my parents and working as a waiter in a restaurant that served breakfast.

Just a few months before everything fell apart, the fantasy was in full swing. The end started with a small tour of England as opening act for a legendary old singer, final arrangements for a new album with my record company were in the works, and I was a member of a supergroup of sorts. But the stench of death was all around. The dream was a lucid one and therefore a more painful illusion. Many lies would have had to be swallowed for the charade to continue. The whole thing was rotten to the core. I didn't have what it takes to climb the ladder.

*Maybe it was the drugs and the visions. Years before I had sat beside a great river during a psychedelic hallucination. It was flowing along as mightily as the old Tigris or the Nile, and it was called the River of Artistic Creation. I realized that one could only sit beside this great river, put a foot in it, swim in it, pray to it, bring people to its banks, but never possess or own it, never dam or pollute it. One should protect it at all costs. At the very least, like the great Ganges, it should remain a sacred place, for all mighty rivers play a profound part in the eternal cycle of life. They are the great connectors. They will carry you. They are a symbol of impermanence in the universe, of perpetual flow, of ultimate freedom.*

Back at the loft I knew I'd better keep the philosophy to myself for a while and swim with the current. We did the tour, it wasn't easy, but I was glad to see the country again. Being back in New York meant no more per diem and I didn't eat much for the first three days. Was I really finished with this life? Probably not. Balance is a hard thing to achieve.

# Manhattan

I'll try to talk very calmly and slowly so you can understand everything that I'm saying to you, I think to myself as I look up at Mana. She's sitting across the table from me and staring straight into my eyes. Her minestrone soup is hot and the steam is rising up into her face. Her back is to the window. I try to speak but before I can get a word out a Harley Davidson with an orange gas tank roars up to the curb and rattles my brain, scrambling my thoughts. I watch as the rider cuts the engine and dismounts.

'So?' Mana wants to know. 'You were saying . . .'

'Oh, nothing really. Yeah, there've been a few. So what? Nothing special, nothing to say really.'

Mana had called this morning, out of nowhere, to see if we could grab lunch together. I told her I was broke and looked like a somnambulist. She said to take a shower and not worry about the money. I was glad and needed to see a familiar face.

When I arrived at Union Square she was already sitting on a step by one of the blue-domed subway entrances, her big brown eyes beaming with delight. We embraced and kissed each other a few times. We've always met here, since the very beginning. We walked south in the cold, smoking her foreign Camel cigarettes, before picking this cozy-looking place to eat.

'Go on,' she says.

I start talking. My spaghetti is steaming, the fragrance of the capers and green olives takes me back to the days when my father was part owner of an Italian restaurant in Dallas: Sweet Basil Ristorante on the southeast corner of Trinity Mills Lane and Midway Road.

'How about a drink?' I blurt out suddenly.

'I thought you wanted to wait?' she says with that sweet motherly voice of hers.

'I need something to make my heart stop beating so goddamned fast,' I say, then try to flag down the waiter.

'Well, so? You were saying about these women?' Mana says.

I try my best to explain the polarity of it all and how unsuited I was for crawling around the flesh piste, that monstrous godforsaken corridor between the East River and the Brooklyn–Queens-Expressway, full of modern-day Minutemen and nymphs with semi-synthetic souls, cunts, cocks, mouths ready to suck, tin-plated hearts, spewing neurotoxic poison from their mouths, thousands of cocks and cunts advancing and retreating to the tunes of the present and the past, sex juice everywhere, slime, trash, rats, vomit, and piss, viscoid and devoid of mystery.

She listens while eating her soup and I can see how much better she has gotten in the eighteen months since our breakup. Not better in a good way but callous enough to handle me talking about other women. When it's her turn she starts right in about her failed attempt at being with a good guy. 'A regular guy,' as she puts it. Irish-Italian, an old schoolmate of hers from the Brooklyn Tech days, an army deserter living with his parents on the Upper West Side, a serious drinker and chain-smoker . . . So far so good.

They reconnected at some funeral, started hanging out, she fell asleep on his bed one night and after waking up at seven or so in the morning found him in the living room with two of his friends doing coke. He had initially sworn he wasn't into drugs.

'At least you are a musician, but he's just an unemployed gas-truck driver. He's got a naked woman in his bed and there he is with two other men doing coke all night?'

Maybe his prick wasn't working at the time, I think.

After a little more storytelling she's ready for a drink too, orders a Bloody Mary. I order a beer. My heart stops beating so fast after a few sips. I hold my hand out in front of her to see if the shakes are gone, and they are.

After a while we finish our meals and drinks, she pays for it, and we walk out into the brutal cold. I'm freezing to death. A few more blocks and I swear I'm going into hypothermic shock.

'The station is close, come on!' she demands.

We quicken our pace, run down the stairs, jump into the train car, find a seat, and scoot in close to one another. We're going to her place, our old place, where it finally fell apart. Where we tried desperately to grasp and clutch to whatever remnants of love existed between us but finally perished, in the dark hours of a cool October morning.

Mana and I get off at 86th Street and take the crosstown to York Avenue, get out and start to walk south. She goes into a deli for a six-pack while I smoke outside. I haven't been near the Upper East Side in a long time but being back in the old neighborhood doesn't affect me in a negative way. This place, the place where she grew up, where I first fell in love with her, a young girl of twenty-one, a recent graduate and living with her parents, vibrant and confused, lovesick and in need of more in her life. Where I looked into her eyes and let her know my feelings and intentions. Where we told her family about us, ate countless dinners and lunches, played kid games with her niece and nephew. Where her mother and sister owned and operated a family daycare in the adjoining apartment. The sister and brother-in-law lived there until they finally bought a place nearby. In a fit of desperation we decided to abandon our Park Slope Brooklyn apartment overlooking the headstones, obelisks, and mausoleums of Greenwood cemetery and move up here since the apartment was cheap and I wasn't bringing in any money.

This charming apartment with its magnificent backyard is where our love crumbled. The final days in this place were full of tempestuous encounters and then finally, as if by design, turbulent winds blew the whole damn charade down to interplanetary dust and the debris was scattered far and wide into our collective futures.

The key is turned, the door is opened, Madam and Monsieur walk in. The place is dark and smells of the past, a deep dark past, a past frozen in time, ingrained in the atoms and cells, an inescapable past full of drama, magic, sorrow, loss, happiness, sex, lonesome yearnings, toenails, lotion, soap suds, contact lenses, cigarettes, laughter, childish games, masturbation, take out, television, dead rotting stinking mice, pain, pain, and love, undying and everlasting. She takes her time taking off her boots, then walks over to the light switch and illuminates the old battlefield.

I walk about the old place. Not much has changed. She goes to the rest room. I move over to the bookshelf and study the old books, every one connected to a time and place. Each title a marker for some distant memory like lying in bed together while we read, or reading on the subway on my way home to see her, or putting down the book to greet her at the door, to embrace and kiss passionately, to take the boots off for her, to rub her legs and hold her for a while. Then she's asking if I want a beer.

We take the beers into her bedroom. She sits on the floor while I study her paintings and drawings that are spread out on a table. She has taken to art since our breakup and the paintings aren't too bad but she gives most of them away foolishly without a signature on the front or back. I pat some of the furniture as if to say hello. Hello again, drawer, hello, closet, hello, table, hello, chair.

I sit on the floor next to her and run my fingers along a boteh pattern on the old Persian rug. Feels nice but the floor is not my favorite place to sit, my ass is all bone. It doesn't take long before we're talking about 'us,' the past, abandonment, having given our best years, why, where, when?

It's getting heated but not out of hand. I'm still sore at her for not adoring me, not making me feel manly enough, not clutching and clawing at me after a great fuck, the same kind of fuck that makes other women melt but used to hardly register a smile from her. Mana says she knows now, has come to realize how good it was.

'Not that I'm admitting to anything,' I say, 'but a man has to prove certain things to himself after a while and, well . . .'

She knows. She knows everything.

The hours roll on as we lie there drinking and listening to Miles Davis, first *Sketches of Spain*, then *Kind of Blue*, then *ESP*. After a while we run out of juice and decide to order some Vietnamese food. She makes me lie down on her bed and lies next to me. The next moment we are holding each other tightly. We still fit. It's incredible how well we fit. I brush her long black hair out of her face and gently caress her cheek with the back of my hand, then grab the back of her head and press her against me. She leans up and kisses me on the lips. I rub her back then gently move down to her legs.

'God, you're so small,' I say.

'You're so small. Where are you? You're so skinny. Just bones,' she says, tapping my hip.

She kisses me again, this time more passionately.

'Come on, the food'll be here soon,' I plead.

'I just put in the order.'

'These Chinamen are fast. That's why they're taking over the world, baby,' I joke in an old-timey voice.

'They're Vietnamese.'

'Charlie's even faster. Back in the shit . . .'

'Come on . . . kiss me . . .'

'Back in 'Nam . . . we used to order lots of Vietnamese.'

'Kiss me.'

'I can't get it out of my mind . . . Damn Vietcong.'

The buzzer goes off. 'You see what I mean?' I say.

'God, how do they make it so fast?'

'They're taking over the goddamn world, I tell ya!'

She leaves to pay for the food and stays in the kitchen for a while preparing a tray and getting more beers.

I start to think about my big idea again, about leaving it all behind and going south, very far south, about the America down there past the equator. The idea has been getting kicked around my brain and endoskeleton for a good while now. There's no shaking it. It's a matter of saving money and breaking free, to book a passage on a ship to Buenos Aires or somewhere like that, to hear the ship's horn, and go out to sea for a spell. To cut the cord and break free, to cleanse myself of the past, to purge, absolve, abandon, destroy, rebuild. I want to scour the earth on a silent quest.

Mana comes back with a tray and I lock away my thoughts as quickly as I had sprung them free. There is no sense in going around in circles. There are lots of loose ends to tie.

'Can we eat in front of the TV? I haven't watched any for so long,' I ask.

'Sure, if you want to,' she says.

We sit on the floor and eat while watching television. When we finish she clears it all away and after a bit of TV we go to bed. We only hold each other, nothing else, and that's fine by me.

*Predynastic Egypt, cuneiform script, Achaemenid commoners, Josephine dancing on a platform in front of a large crowd like Esmeralda. She sees me standing amongst the mob. We lock eyes. She stops dancing and looks frightened. She starts screaming but her voice is inaudible. She reaches out to me, arms fully extended with palms out. In a flash she is holding a newborn infant; the umbilical cord is still attached to it and to her as well, it's a blood-soaked mess. The baby is not breathing. It is dead.*

My cell phone buzzes. I reach over and silence it. Mana is fast asleep. After washing my face over the bathroom sink I study it in the mirror for a moment with a sly appreciation. 'Not bad, not bad,' I say aloud, mimicking Dustin Hoffman as Ratso Rizzo in *Midnight Cowboy*. 'Beautiful Baby . . . you're beautiful. Can't you try and love yourself? Can't you do that for me?' I continue. 'You should have stayed in LA and really gone after it, you fool. You could've been a star, a star I tell ya . . . Na, fuck LA.'

I don't wake Mana up to say goodbye but stand there for a minute and look over her slumbering body. Whatever dreams she's wrapped up in will not be remembered. She's out for the count. Not once did she recall a dream of hers to me in the six years we were together. She expires and yields to that distant finality, vanishes from the sphere of consciousness altogether, departs this world and the other one too. Good for her, I say. For me dreams are a part of my memories and accompany me in my waking life. We are married, united, confederated, allied, my dreams and I. Chromatic dreams they are, mostly sordid little episodes, sometimes melodious but often discordant, full of tonal modulations and demonic visions, fiendish and guilt-ridden.

I walk out the door and brace myself against the brutal cold. What a winter we've had. All snowfall records were broken this year. I quicken my pace and recall my dream from earlier. I wonder what Josephine is up to. She must be thinking about me. That's the third time this week she has visited me in a dream. Is she here in New York? I wonder if she married that rich Arab from the Emirates. Did he give her that Avenue Montaigne apartment in Paris or did he take her back to Dubai?

I try to forget Josephine and concentrate on my gastric needs. Coffee, but not the expensive kind I love so much. No, stick to the cheap stuff. Why didn't I ask

Mana to lend me some money? I was definitely broke again. How was I going to get through the month? First things first, coffee then go home and see about getting stoned, then call Carter and beg for my old job back. Go back to the graveyard shift. Go rot in that glossy office building through the night.

The first sip of coffee puts a smile on my face, and then a few women check me out on the subway platform and this makes a positive impression on me. What the hell? I think. What's wrong about it all? Nothing, that's what. Are you starving? Do you have an incurable illness? It's all dollars and cents. Problems? What problems? One foot in front of the other, Ali, step, step, step. One, two, three, four, two, two, three, four. What you need now is a hot shower and a big fat joint. A few hours of playing music and it'll be night time before you know it.

# Brooklyn

While making my way on foot down to the Williamsburg Bridge I get a phone call from Michael. I met him a few weeks ago at some lame party full of yuppie screwheads. It was one of those parties I go to when an old friend begs me to spend some time with them, knowing there will be an endless supply of free booze to keep me happy. My friend Lexi had invited me. She is an old friend from the Dallas theater days, a real fine gal, nice dimples, shapely thighs, a late bloomer. There were all kinds of dull conversations echoing off the walls.

Michael introduced himself to me and said he was a painter, just back from a solo show in Berlin, a rich boy from the little bit I could gather, summers in the south of France, winters in the Swiss Alps and what have you. He took a liking to me, maybe because of my bad attitude. Sometimes my drunken sulking sourpuss rude manner is amusing to people, especially hotshots who get their asses kissed all day long. Anyway he said he'd heard of me from Lexi, said he heard I was an incredible singer and stuff like that. I think he's bisexual, which is fine by me. He's rich and I need a meal. What a stroke of good luck.

I tell the doorman who I'm seeing and take the elevator up to Michael's apartment. It's in one of those brand new high-rises by the Hudson. These places make me want to puke. The door opens and I'm greeted by a tall impeccably dressed woman talking on her cell phone.

'The last thing anybody wants is another disaster like that. Why would he? That's no kind of reason. Well I'd say pull on anybody's . . . Just make sure he's guaranteed the right amount upfront . . . and . . . and . . . that the PR is up to standard. We're not responsible if . . .' she's saying.

I follow the woman around the spacious apartment decorated in an ultra-hip fashion with lots of modern art hanging on the walls. In the living room Michael is taking photos of two young women who are barely wearing any clothes. It's some kind of Grecian summer's eve scene or it could be the children of Ophir delivering Solomon's gold, I can't tell. The girls are very attractive, model types, statuesque beauties wearing Tyrian purple-dyed capes. Michael stops taking photos for a moment to greet me.

'Hello, old friend, how are you? Did you meet Barbara?' he says, motioning towards the phone talker.

'Hello, no I didn't. Hi, Barbara,' I say, but Barbara is busy with her conversation.

'Well, what do you think? Nice, ha?' he says, motioning towards the girls with his head, hands holding his camera.

'Yeah, hello . . .' I say to the girls but they don't break character. They're no slouches these two. Look like they have careers in modeling.

'Well, make yourself at home, grab a drink, a beer, whatever, I know you like to drink, so just grab anything you like, do anything you like. We should be done here in a little bit then we can do lunch.'

'Okay, thanks, I will.' I walk around to the kitchen and open the fridge, it's full of the best a man can buy, and choose a nice Czech beer.

A little while later we're all sitting around a table with food and drinks. Michael's telling a story about meeting Warhol. I don't care if he's bullshitting or not. I don't give a fuck what he says.

'No, I didn't know him, I was just a kid. It was like a little bit before he died, I don't ever talk about it . . . Guess I hadn't been home every other time he'd come over or something, I don't know. Whatever, so I just said, "Mommy, what's wrong with that man's hair? I really like it," and she just laughed it off, you know.'

'What did he say?' one of the models wants to know.

'He said something like, "Gee, Elaine, your boy's a real pain in the neck, but he's got a marvelous face," or something like that. Anyway, that's my story,' says

Michael, his voice becoming more and more effeminate with every sip of his drink.

He turns the music up real loud, I recognize it after a few bars: it's Ravel's *Bolero*, of all things. He starts chasing one of the girls around. They disappear into another room and after a few minutes return carrying a big trunk, open it, and start trying on different kinds of costumes. Barbara is still on the phone and completely oblivious to the whole scene. I'm sitting on a couch drinking, with the other model talking to me in a rapid-fire way. We've gotten into the coke that Michael put on the coffee table in front of us.

'She had herself a real good time in Milan, up for a couple of days straight. Hey! Watch it, you two, this is my favorite dress. God, they make a nice pair, don't they? Wait till she gets her whips and chains out on the poor bastard. She likes to really hurt and be hurt, you know what I'm talking about? Do you? She's gotten me into it too recently, taught me a few tricks, minor things. You know you can make a pretty good living whipping rich men. Not that we do that or anything. What I don't get is the ball-stomp thing. What is the joy in that? I mean, a good hard spanking or whipping fine, but high heels on testes?'

She's going on and on like that and I'm trying for the life of me to remember her name. Waste Land Eyes, I decide to call her. She has a soft creamy complexion, reminds me of a young Gene Tierney, her voice is sardonically barren and monotone, her vermilion soul is giving me the creeps. I don't want to stay here all night and watch these fools act out their lives in front of me.

The model keeps talking and I turn my eye into a camera focusing on different parts of her body. She is beautiful if nothing else. My camera focuses on her lips, moves down her neck, past her small shapely breasts, follows the contours of her leg, from her thigh down to her foot, toe cleavage and all, then back up and under her skirt, undressing her, and throwing a silent fuck into her. Suddenly her bare mid-section flashes on the screen, she is holding a lit cigarette, the smoke is curling up, her dark hair falls down her back, her blinking wasteland eyes stare blankly ahead, she walks towards a wall slowly raising her arms and places both palms on the wall, her head turns, her lips blow a kiss. My film runs out and the camera stops.

I find myself in the bathroom splashing water on my face, intent on getting the hell out of there as soon as I can. When I get out of the bathroom Waste Land Eyes is waiting for me, grabs my hand and takes me into one of the rooms, walks me to the middle, lets go of my hand, walks to the door, closes it, turns and walks towards me slowly. She stands before me and without a word grabs my hand and guides it up her leg and under her skirt to her engorged centre. She's not wearing anything under there and it's hot enough to burn my fingers. I move my fingers around slowly, she grabs my bicep and clinches, digging her crimson-colored nails into me. The pain makes me angry, I plunge a finger deep into her. She lets out a devilish moan, grabs my crotch and squeezes a hard grunt out of me.

'What's the matter? Can't take it?' she says with a diabolical smile forming upon her face. I don't say a word, if this is the game then so be it. If the scene requires a rough fuck with a stranger on a strange night then what choice do I have, right? But something about this doesn't seem right to me and my mind starts to drift. She notices this and gives me a hard slap in the face. Violence is not my thing. I disengage and walk to the door.

'What?' she says, short of breath, with mouth in mid-contortion. 'What are you doing?'

'I'm not doing this.'

'What? You were doing it!' she says angrily.

'I was and now I'm not.'

'Is this a fucking joke? Are you crazy? Do you know how many men would kill to be doing what you're doing right now, asshole?'

'Yes, I do. Quite a few. Most probably. I'm sorry, I can't go through with it.'

'You stupid fuck! Fuck you!' she screams.

I leave the room as quickly as possible, trot through the apartment, out the door, down the stairs, and into the street. I don't plan on seeing any of those people ever again and with some luck won't ever have to. Not my crowd.

The streets are humming with an energy that can produce an arc of electricity at any moment. I'm walking in a vector field of people and seeing everything in shades of nickel antimony titanium yellow. A part of the degenerate human race eternal I am, no better and no worse than anybody else, with a full belly and a full mind walking through New York City. Not the first wretched fool or the last, of that we can all be sure.

The important things to remember are the simple things, the little things, the here and now things, the small words, slight differences in tone and attitude, pressure changes, pitch changes, what the eyes say, what the mouth doesn't say. Collections of memories to transport to the next day and next life, ciphers from your past selves to your future selves, the present self will have to be the one hunting, farming, collecting, bending, scooping, begging, pleading, fighting, pissing people off, et cetera, ad infinitum.

I open the door to the loft and walk in. It's quiet. Someone is asleep on my bed with the covers pulled over his or her head. My bed is in the middle of the loft and easily accessible to visitors. Siamak is the lead singer of the band and he made the bed for me as a birthday gift. I look closer to see who the sleeper is. It's Dari again. The bastard's been spending a hell of a lot of time on my bed lately. He's a freeloader of the highest order, though in his defence his immigration status doesn't allow him to work legally. He comes over and stays for a week. Likes to time his visits on days when the kids are going food shopping, then stays and cooks our favorite meals for a few days. Of course our favorite meals are really his favorite meals and he has a heavy hand with the expensive ingredients like saffron, which the kids get sent over from Iran. He acts like a master chef and basically just orders people around in a rude yet funny manner while tasting and adding spices.

As if that weren't enough he smokes our cigarettes and invites women over and uses our beds. He's a metronomic, long-distance fucker too and really makes these girls sing like the whorish devil birds they really are. He roams around looking like a goddamn bum until it's time for a meeting with one of these birds, then undergoes a transformation fit for a Persian king of the Sassanid period. Being Iranian, hair removal is the most important part of his transmutation. He must also be oiled from head to toe. I keep telling him about chest hair being back in style but he won't listen. His beard must be shaved in a certain pattern and trimmed to perfection. He's always talking about potential threesomes but nothing ever pans out.

'Oh, her!' he exclaims. 'She's totally the type! Let's have an orgy with her.'

Dari also likes to think of himself as a sort of intellectual. He speaks with a pseudo-English accent, although he grew up in Iran. He's a musician, came over with the first wave of Iranian underground rock bands. Most of his one-liners are recycled Woody Allen lines or something he might have picked up from Camus or Dostoevsky, and he likes to lay it on thick and go real slow without citing his sources. Well, come to think of it, his wild ideas do pan out sometimes, and his intellectual mumbo-jumbo does impress some more than others. Truth is, last time I saw Dari his face was buried in a cunt, sucking and licking. The cunt had a face, arms, and legs, blond hair and blue eyes. I was engaged with her upper body, a nipple in my mouth, eyes fixed on her lower torso. She was enjoying herself, very much so. Her boyfriend was not present on this fortuitous night, had elected to stay far away on the other side of town, the dumb bastard. If he only knew what kind of depraved monsters were pleasuring his girlfriend.

After two or three tall glasses of absinthe on the rocks with a splash of water human beings will try anything. I don't have to have orgies to get my blood flowing but rather enjoy doing the deed with one person at a time in a semi-sober fashion. It was an empty experience. Not primordial in nature. Ephemeral and vacuous. One for the vault of human degeneracy and corruption, animalistic, and devoid of poetry. I should have walked away from it the second it started. We looked like the octopuses in Hokusai's *The Dream of the Fisherman's Wife*, God help us. To make things even worse the girl was a friend of mine.

Unlike me, Dari is a genuine sex addict of the highest order, a serval, a serotine bat, a self-professed coitus king, a deflowering inseminator, a penetrator, a copulating land shark with a powerful appetite for flesh. One day he will surely have a symposium on the art of coition and defend his points like Plato. I assume he is gathering all the necessary data now for this future sparging of knowledge and wisdom. Soon he will retire to one of the Balearic Islands off the coast of Spain to ponder his findings with a hermit's zeal and a solitudinarian's fervency. He says I can visit him there anytime I like, and why the hell not? I could use some sun and sand.

I light a cigarette and stare out the window. All is frozen in the mercury dawn, steam is rising from the chimney tops, a few birds in the sky, looks like it'll snow. It's up and down all the time. I need to slow it down, get a job, some solitude and rest. Can't keep running. Must keep running. I slide in bed next to Dari, without touching him of course, and try to get a few hours of sleep before the loft's inhabitants awaken from their slumber. I need to shut off my mind for a spell. Please, Lord, no dreams and no nightmares. My mind starts to wander again . . .

Oh but what shall remain of my infinite pipe dreams? So many dreams, so many ideas that die once chewed on or exclaimed. For every door you open another shuts in your face. There are very few streets to walk down, very few roads to travel. The entirety of this city, country, and world even has been made to fit into this hand-sized magic device named after the fruit Adam and Eve couldn't resist, which contains almost all that has ever been written, recorded, and filmed by man. All the supposed knowledge of the known universe is held within, without the wisdom of course, without care, and entirely for profit. Children barely able to speak are handed these terrible devices to idle away their time. God forbid the young should experience brief periods of boredom and bother their overwrought parents, better to let the children look into the abyss of the magic machines and shut up. With the magic comes wave after wave of arresting codes, spells of maddening numbness, mind programming, mining of the soul, dulling of the senses, easy slavery, from womb to slaughter. A soul/spirit slaughter complete with parental supervision, guidance, and permission signed on the dotted line. 'We'd be happy to!' the parents say. 'We love your product. We use it ourselves.' Oh, just shut up and go to sleep, you fool, I think. You're lucky to be here at all, you damn dirty immigrant. You've got a roof over your head and a pot to piss in, be happy.

When I wake the loft is in full swing. Dari's cooking and yapping on about the girl he had the previous night. The kids are listening and rolling a joint.

'Her face was disgusting, she was so fucking stupid, her feet stank a little too,' he's saying in Farsi.

'How did you meet her?' asks Koli, the bass player.

'She was at one of our shows a while back. Listen, I'm pretty sure we can do an orgy with her, none of you guys were around last night or it would have happened. She liked to get spanked. God she was a dumb bitch, was buying me drinks all night, rich girl, trust-fund girl, from Missouri or somewhere like that, maybe Michigan, I don't give a fuck. She was a good enough lay though. I made her come five or six times and she still wanted more. Wanted me to put it in her ass. Where's the saffron?'

I stare out the window and wait for the bathroom to free up.

'Ali! Thanks for letting me sleep on your bed last night. Man, you don't move at all when you sleep, like you're dead.'

'I am dead, Dari, dead in the heart.'

'Goddamned dark bastard! Lighten up. Just wait till you taste what I'm cooking for you guys. Let's eat this and hit the streets. I'm gonna cheer you up,' he says, clapping, then wringing his hands together.

'What do you have in mind?' I ask.

'There's gotta be an open bar somewhere. You gotta get good and wasted before you leave to join that cult, don't you?'

'Eh . . . I don't know. I hate open bars.'

'Well why don't you call up that friend of yours, what's her name, from the other night? The Croatian girl.'

'Goddamn you, Dari. Why don't *you* call her, you pimp bastard, didn't you get her number? What do you need me for?'

'You're right, she wasn't that good anyway. It wouldn't be any fun without you.'

'Yeah, well. I'm never doing that again,' I say.

'Oh, come on! You're telling me you didn't like it?'

'No, I didn't like it. You're fucking sick, you know that?'

'Look it's not *my* fault mine is bigger than yours, is it?' he says with a laugh.

'No, you're right, it's not your fault.'

'Well, it's pretty big isn't it?' he says with a triumphant ear-to-ear smile.

'Yeah, it's pretty big for a condor. You know, unlike other species of new world vultures, though, your kind is not endangered but flourishing.'

'Well, what do you want me to do, be like you and pass up a good carcass when I see one? If I am a condor, like you say I am, then I can't help myself, right? That's just my nature.'

'Well done, Dari, that's the first sensible thing I've heard you say all month. Now is this goddamn food ready or what? And take it easy with our saffron.'

After a while we sit around the large wooden dining table and enjoy Dari's Ghormeh Sabzi, a favorite dish of most Iranians. He really is a master in the kitchen.

'You son of a bitch, you're the best goddamn cook ever, this is the best I've ever had,' I say.

'Yeah, Dari, wow!' Koli concurs, as do all the others with noises and nods.

'Did you learn this from your mother or what?' asks Manuchehr, the lead guitarist.

'Hell, no!' Dari says. 'She couldn't even fry an egg. I started cooking when we came to America . . . out of desperation.'

These family meals are a daily occurrence at the loft. Besides a main dish we have to have plain yogurt, a salad of some kind, either Coca-Cola or beer if possible. After the meal: cigarettes and a joint.

While we're smoking Dari tells us a story about his old cat, which he used to walk like a dog on the streets of Tehran. One day there was a fight caused by the cat that involved a truckload of construction workers with axes and shovels.

'The judge says to me, "Why did you hit the guy?" I said because he hit my cat, he saw the cat, said, "Cat," and hit it with a shoe! "Cat?" says the judge. "Hit your cat? That's what you're supposed to do to cats," he says! Can you believe that! What kind of a shithole country? I mean . . .'

Our cat is fat and lazy but great for the girls. We smoke our joint and scatter. I start to strum my guitar, Dari gets a phone call from someone. It's getting dark out and the night will have to be filled up with some kind of entertainment.

The door opens and some people one of the kids had met the night before walk in. Before long others arrive and we're drinking and smoking, talking about ordering cocaine. The dealer turns up after a while. Why the hell we can't do something useful with our lives is beyond me. We have all the necessary tools and manpower at our disposal but we choose to ignore the real things and contribute to the nonsense.

'I won't play any Stravinsky but I'll play you some Schubert,' Carrie says while getting up and going over to the piano.

'Now, this is a piece I'm learning so it won't be perfect,' she says, before plunging into it with full force. She has incredible technique, powerful fingers yet delicate hands, and is deep inside the music. She plays eloquently and with intense feeling. She looks very sexy in her tight jeans, high rising brown boots, and tight long-sleeve sweater. Her short blondish-brown hair sways back and forth as she pounds the keys. I laugh out loud uncontrollably at some of the passages in the composition. I'm drunk and stoned, the coke has probably worn off by now.

She's taking me out of my diminished self and into the phantasmal world where kaleidoscopic images sparkle in all directions at once. Her back arched, her mind alert, she toys with my senses, imploring, cajoling, ridiculing, ostracizing. Electromagnetic waves oscillate longitudinally in the free space between us. My thoughts flow freely and drift towards optics, seismology, telecommunications, wave propagation, magnetic fields, vectors, amplitude, phase, sinusoidal waves, angular frequency, harmonics, timbre, synchrotron radiation, length contraction. The music retards suddenly and gives way to new thought streams. Now I'm in Ciudad de Mexico walking around Centro Historico. I'm in the floating gardens of Xochimilco. I can see Zocalo in the distance, castle of Chapultepec, Coyoacan, Frida, Diego, Trotsky, ghosts. I am swimming in the music, bathing in it, drinking it all in. Watching her now, young, vibrant, independent, comfortable in her own skin. The music ends and leaves me stranded in the middle of an imagined cathedral. She looks over at me, smiling.

'That's it! I'm still working on it,' she says.

'God, Carrie, that was beautiful. You are amazing,' I say.

'Thank you,' she says as she gets up from the piano stool to walk over and sit beside me. She looks at me and smiles, her eyes bluer than lapis lazuli, then puts her head on my shoulder as if we'd known each other for years. I let her keep it there for a while then lift her chin up with my forefinger and kiss her on the lips. She kisses me back passionately. We are in no hurry.

My thoughts are flowing again. *Predynastic Egypt, cuneiform script, Grand Anicut, Sumer, Elam, Babylonian captivity, Achaemenid commoners.* Her thoughts are her own and I have no way of knowing where her mind is. She is becoming more and more aroused. My hand is under her sweater now and feeling her pale skin. I kiss and bite her neck. She moans as a wave washes over her body then stops suddenly.

'Wait . . . okay, wait a minute . . . Now I like you, I do, but I'm not gonna fuck you tonight . . . If you want, though, we can go to the bedroom and get a little more comfortable?'

'Sure, whatever you like,' I say, knowing exactly what's going to happen if we go to the bedroom. We lie on her bed with our clothes on for a while and continue to go at it slowly. I am not in a great hurry so let her lead the way. She takes off her sweater and asks me to take off mine, then the shirts, her bra, our jeans, and eventually the underwear. After a while I ask if she'd like for me to go down on her and she nods her head, Yes, eyes halfway shut, her tongue rolling over her lips, her teeth biting her lower lip, she's ready for it. I start to make my way down calmly, meticulously kissing and licking her body on the way before making final contact. I look up at her, her body is squirming with pleasure, her back is arched, nipples erect, head back, her eyes are closed, she's moaning. I reach up and squeeze her left breast, then play with her erect pink nipple in between my fingers. After a few minutes I stick a finger in gently and move it in and out while I massage her with my tongue. She's going crazy now.

'Stop! Okay! . . . Let's stop for a second,' she says, completely out of breath, and pulls me up and makes me hold her.

After a moment I disengage to rest my head on the wall behind the bed, pour myself a drink from the bottle of single malt Scotch on the mantelpiece, and take a long sip. 'I'll be right back,' she says, and goes to the bathroom.

Why I'm in bed with her is a mystery to me. When the loft door opens anyone could walk in from anywhere in the world. I didn't even notice her until the end of the night. It's always so dark in there. She came up to me, asked for a cigarette, looked good enough, we talked for a little while, she flirted with her eyes, I kept my cool, wasn't in a very good mood, didn't want to talk to anybody, just wanted to do my coke and hang out with the kids. Carrie went away after a few bumps of my coke and I saw her giving the same kind of attention to a few other guys. I'm not falling for their shit anymore, I was thinking. The nicer you are to these girls the worse they treat you. Gentlemen, it seems, get the short end of the stick. I just let her do her thing and didn't even look at her for an hour or so until she came back and started talking to me again, said she'd found a pack of cigarettes in the bathroom, and gave me one before accepting another bump. We started talking again, this time about music. She's a classically trained pianist. We talked about Schoenberg and Stravinsky, Strauss and Satie. After a while she disappears again and when I locate her, it looks for a second as if she's kissing some guy. Next time I see her she's asking if I want to go to her place and smoke some pot. Now here we are. I pour myself another Scotch neat and wait for Carrie to come out of the bathroom. She comes out naked and smiling.

'Hi,' she says.

'Hey,' I say. She gets in bed and slides close to me. Her left hand slips down and grabs it.

'What are you doing?' she asks.

'Just waiting for you.'

'Waiting for me, ha?'

'Yeah, what were you doing in there?'

'Girl stuff.'

'Hmm . . .'

'Come on . . .'

She's turned on, starts to stroke it harder, I slip a finger into her and she's ready for me in a flash.

'Get a condom,' I say.

'No, no sex,' she says.

No sex, you fool? You liar, I think to myself as I move my middle finger in and out of her. A few more minutes of that and she's ready for anything, leans forward and opens a drawer to get a condom out.

'Put it on me,' I say to her, and she does, then grabs my cock and sits on me. I grab her waist and move her up and down. She leans forward and sticks her tongue down my throat. I bite her lower lip then grab a breast and suck on her nipple. She leans back and arches. I move up and grab her upper back then bury my face in her tits. A moment later she's on her stomach and I'm fucking her like a dog. There is not an ounce of love in my soul. I have no sympathy for her vulnerabilities nor my own, nor anybody else's. I know her kind, she will not be in my life past tonight, nor does she want to be. Hell, I don't know a goddamned thing about her. God only knows who else she does this with and how many times a week. I am pounding away as she moans and groans. I turn her around and give it to her missionary style with emphatic repetition. She comes after a few minutes but I don't stop to let her take a breather. Fuck you! I think. I know your kind. You get it while you can and so will I.

I hammer away and feel the pressure building, feel the little soldiers on the march, see the Hanging Gardens of Babylon pulverized by the cannon of a gunship. I am now a beast, should be sacrificed to the gods, just a brute with nothing but common blood in his veins. My ancestors were raped by Mongols! Kill this vermin if you dare! If you know what's good for you! I will fuck your mother, your daughter, your sister, I'll fuck *you* till you bleed, you son of a bitch! I will act domesticated but just as soon as you turn your head this little pet will turn into a scavenger, a moulter shedding my outer skin and darting for the bleeding flesh. I ain't no purebred but a stayer nevertheless. Fuck you, I'm a mutant! I am the opposite of whatever you think I am. If land proves too difficult then the sea is where I'll go. I am cruel, Carrie, I think to myself, much more cruel than you, but you win, you win.

She seems to have enjoyed herself. I feel like a

wretched fool. We fall asleep together for a few hours until day breaks, then I wake up and leave. It's brutally cold and I've got a long walk back to the loft, the kids will want to know the story when they wake up in the evening and will have a few stories of their own. We'll talk about who fucked who and who didn't, then the day will pass into night and into day again. I feel pathetic. There are all kinds of proposals on the table, tours, projects, shows, and whatnot. I need love. I don't want this jumping from branch to branch, don't want to become what I'm becoming.

'Hey, man, can I buy a cigarette from you?' some rat-faced bastard with a nice smile and an expensive haircut asks me.

'Don't have any, man, sorry,' I say while walking past him.

Too many confounding questions haunt me on this useless walk. There isn't a drug in the world that can cure my ills. All change must come from within but my insides feel rotten and disturbed. I feel like a soft-headed screwball or an impractical eccentric walking down a peculiar looking corridor with hanging curtains in my face. I slowly brush the curtains aside with a quixotic look and discover nothing but absurdity and ridiculousness.

'Just a little farther,' I say with an idiotic grin and keep on. 'Hello!' I croak. 'Is there anybody there?' If only I had learned to be more provident. When will

I find a way out of this deranged corridor? Is there nothing else? How many peaks and valleys must I traverse? There is so much I wish to convey to the people around me, some inner significance that I grasp with every fiber of my being, but cannot put into words. There must be a correct gesture, some subtle nuance or symbol to help me communicate my intent.

'Explicate, damn you!' I scream into space. I desperately need clarity and resolution. I feel like a stowaway on my own ship and after wandering out from the bowels of the vessel find it devoid of passengers. Upon closer observation I begin to have doubts regarding the seaworthiness of the craft. The steerage seems shot, the bilge well is overflowing, the sternpost is broken in half, the stokehole is without fire, and worst of all the escutcheon does not display a name. An ungodly wave is swelling out there, the dark sea is angry, a sudden great rise is building, and a billow is on its way towards my broken ship. The sky turns black as storm clouds roll in, heavy rain, lightning and thunder. The wind howls a menacing tune, and overwhelms my senses. I brace myself for the final end, but somehow know that it isn't coming anytime soon. I know that the ship will surely capsize, but somehow I will not drown. No, it will not be that easy. After the vessel is gone there still remains the sea, and thousands of islands to wash ashore onto. So brace yourself, sailor, we've got lots of swimming ahead of us.

I walk into the loft. Manuchehr is up and making himself some tea. We sit at the table. I pick up my guitar and strum an Appalachian-sounding tune.

'Last night was crazy,' he says.

'What happened with that girl?' I ask.

'Nothing with her, but I got it on with that old woman,' he says with a vulnerable smile.

'Old woman? Which old woman? How old was she?'

'I don't know, maybe thirty.'

'Jesus, I'm thirty-two, are you calling me old?' I ask with a smirk.

'Eh . . . no. She was a funny one though, I was at it for at least two hours once it started, God these women are so weird, it's always the ones who pretend not to care, we didn't say a word to each other all night.'

'Well, they like you 'cause you're quiet,' I say.

'Yeah, I guess so . . . it always happens at the last minute for me. She came into my room to do some coke, then just stayed. We weren't even talking, people coming in and out. We didn't say a word to each other, hours passed, everyone left. Finally I say I'm tired and want to get some sleep. She says go ahead but lies down beside me. We start making out and it's getting heavy, but she keeps stopping and saying that's enough every five minutes. So I just say okay every time and turn around as if I'm going to sleep. Of course she starts back up every time, finally I just say, Look, this is dumb, grab her and we go at it. We did it for hours, sweat dripping. Finally we get done and she starts asking me questions. Like, What do you do? I say I'm in a band, like she didn't know. She says, But what do you do for money? I say, That's it, I don't do anything for money. She says, But you have a job, right? I say, I've never had a job. She starts to get pissed off, says, What, never had a job, ever? I say, No. She gets seriously pissed now, says she's been working since she was fourteen, has three jobs right now just to support herself, and can't imagine somebody not working. She gets up and starts gathering all her things to leave. Just before she walks out she stops, turns, and tells me . . . to get a job!'

'Ha! Get a job?' I ask, laughing.

'Yeah! Get a job.'

Just then Koli walks out of his room, feet dragging, looking like a ghost but smiling from ear to ear. He sits down and gets in on the conversation.

'My God . . . my God,' he keeps saying while shaking his head.

'What is it? Are you all right?' I ask him.

'My God . . .'

'Koli, spit it out. What the fuck happened?'

'She is a goddamn goddess. Is this heaven? Am I in fucking heaven right now? I mean, the body, the tits alone . . . just the goddamn body, and her face!'

He is totally cunt-struck, hysterical, his eyes are popped out, and he can't stop shaking his head.

'Which one?' I ask.

'The Danish one. She's around your age, and my God . . . I'm in love,' he says, flinging his hands up into the air then slamming them down on his knees.

'Where is she?' Manuchehr asks.

'She left, said it was too bright in my room for her to sleep. I'm buying some curtains today, damn it. She's the one. I mean, how can a woman's body look and feel like that? She made me a man, I was just a boy until last night. She made a man out of me . . . My God.'

He is in a trance, there's no use talking to him now. Surely he will stay that way for a week or more. Every once in a while a girl comes along with a golden, magical, supernatural, paranormal, phantasmagorical vagina, one which erases all memories of previous vaginas. Koli seems to have come across one of these surrealistic vaginas and it has completely fried his circuitry. The top of his head is about to blow off. He is in a world of trouble now because those vaginas are attached to a living, breathing human being of the female sex and not some abstract concept. A man doesn't have sex with, make love to, fuck, marry, or divorce a vagina but another human being. Cock or cunt makes no difference. Above the sex is the other stuff. If you wish to enter the realm of life eternal, which you are already a part of anyway, then you must understand certain elementary concepts. You know if you fuck the right way babies get made, don't you? Babies are alive. They *are* life. It's a big thing this fucking and sucking. It's the end all, be all of it all. No bullshit.

Tomorrow at dawn I leave for a meditation camp. At this camp no one is allowed to speak, or kill, eat meat, smoke, drink, fuck, or write, sing, dance, run, work out, etc. It's free detox for people like myself who can proudly call themselves addicts, drug addicts to be exact, and an alcoholic to boot. Oh, and if I could, that is if I could afford it in New York City, I would smoke two to three packs of cigarettes a day, but cigarettes being almost thirteen dollars per pack makes it difficult to fully indulge.

The most peculiar feelings are rushing through me tonight. I have no idea what it is that I'm feeling. I only know that I'm okay with everything in my life. I am still frightened and cannot possibly know what's around the corner but am experiencing a calm that I have not experienced in a long time. I hope to have some magical visions.

You can't explain it really. What can you say about a meditation camp and the teachings of the twenty-eighth Buddha, Siddhartha Gautama? For twelve straight days I was living like a monk, eating simple vegetarian meals, observing noble silence – which consists of no communication whatsoever with anyone else at the camp – waking up at 4 a.m. to sounds of gently ringing Tibetan bells, meditating for almost six hours during the day, walking around the grounds or sleeping the rest of the time, and by lights out at 10 p.m. gearing up for hellish dreams, which meant visits from past girlfriends and lost loves, demonic visions and sounds echoing within my inner mass and being heard and felt with more intensity than ever before due to the heightened senses.

Every being I've ever come into contact with seemed to visit me in my many dreams. My legs were pure mush from sitting in the lotus position without moving for hours upon hours and woke me up with convulsions at regular intervals throughout the night. My sleeping quarters were inside one of about ten small wooden cabins built to house four meditators each, but after the others left I enjoyed a whole cabin to myself, which wasn't anything elegant, just a bed and a chair.

The only thing to do for fun was walk around the grounds, which were basically the woods and rather beautiful, or to lie there on your bed and let the mind wander. A lot of people dropped out and left the place to go back to the outside world. Among them was a full-fledged monk who we had to respectfully allow first-eating rights, the bald bastard. I would have left too but didn't have money for a bus fare back to New York and was planning on getting a ride from an enlightened individual on the last day.

The one person I wish had left early was this ugly-looking young rat bastard who proceeded to burp and fart in my direction on a daily basis for a reaction, but the whole point of the Vipassana meditation technique is to teach a person to remain equanimous and not react with craving or aversion to anything as impermanent as a fart or burp, therefore he received no reaction from me. I felt like throwing the son of a bitch down the cliff overlooking the creek but had to remain non-violent for obvious reasons.

To categorically dismiss problems, solutions, equations, elucidations, and questions is a thing of the past for me now. Why not transcend all negativity? It is hard not to react to sensations with craving and/or aversion but one must try. I don't intend to practice teetotalism in any way but the ancient and universal concept of moderation will have to be observed on some level if I am to continue on a forward path leading to a long life in this body. I knew all of this before of course.

The kids and I are smoking a joint and talking about Iran. Manuchehr is telling me about the time he got robbed at knifepoint in a taxi, also about them traveling to Hengam Island in the Persian Gulf, doing acid, laying down on a rock when the ground started to move because of an earthquake, and freaking out, naturally. There's a knock at the door, it's the surrogate landlord. He's a tall, handsome, mustachioed, Swiss devil, very nice and cordial.

'Hello, guys, how's it going?' says the Swiss. He always comes in right after we light a joint, can sense it, and supposedly they don't know about *puff-puff-give* in Switzerland, it's *puff-puff-puff, hold, puff-puff-hold* until the joint is finished.

'Have some bad news . . . we'll have to be out in two months,' he says. We've been waiting for this bad news for a while. The city is eliminating these kinds of dwellings for good. No more industrial-zoned buildings will be able to house people without first kicking everyone out, re-zoning, and charging astronomically high rents.

'So start looking for a new place immediately,' he

says in his charming lightly accented German voice.

Our landlord is just a guy who rents from the actual owner of the building. He has had the lease for years, lives in Southeast Asia, been there for a long time, can't come back to the States because of some old crime or something. Our Swiss friend takes care of the building in exchange for free rent. He also owns a small art gallery down the street. We haven't had hot water for a week and the bathtub is filled with sewer gunk but at least the Swiss isn't asking about the rent, which is three weeks past due.

'What the hell are we supposed to do now?' asks Siamak after the Swiss leaves.

'Look for another place, obviously,' Koli says.

This is a big blow and we need something to help us relax. After a quick meeting we decide it will be a Tramadol night. Tramadol is a synthetic opiate that is very popular among drug users in the old country. The kids introduced me to it. If you take enough it can feel very close to heroin. The lights need to be dim and the music soothing. You need plenty of sweetened hot tea, no phones, no disturbances, and no shrieking sounds. Just lie down somewhere and drift off into the abyss. We have a Hungarian doctor friend who prescribes it to us. He's a proctologist by trade and we have, after all, many gastrointestinal conditions to ameliorate. Musicians need a good rectal exam every once in a while to make sure all is in working order, rectally speaking.

He'd make house calls often as he is an old-school gent, a real hoot and a holler too, a showman who is older and wiser than the rest of us with a steady and warm hand.

His medical opinions were for us like scripture. It wasn't just his absolute and encyclopedic knowledge of the anus and sphincter which was of use to us, no, we went to him for all other medical needs as well. Doctor, my tooth is really hurting back there . . . Hey, Doc, can you take a look at this here, yeah, right around the shaft? Doctor, if she's all the way in Iowa, and it was only one night, is it still my responsibility? Doc, am I growing? Doc, what does it mean when you wake up in the middle of the night, in a cold sweat, breathing heavily, and don't know who you are, like have no idea, is that amnesia?

He was a poet the good doctor, would sit there by your side, on the bed, and speak of anything and everything from astrophysics to geology. He was at home discussing all the natural sciences, but he really liked to compare the internal workings of humans with dark matter. How we needed him in those days and how well he performed. God, Universe, Mother Earth, bless our good friend the Hungarian doctor, for he was our Avicenna.

Infinite wisdom hidden below and above or not hidden at all but smiling and waving, beckoning. We were never hungry growing up, that much is true. I didn't know real hunger until I struck out on my own. There was real romance in it at first. So many great artists have gone hungry. Fasting, they told us in school back in Iran, is a sort of conduit to the reality of the poor. One finds out only too soon, however, how devoid of romance involuntary hunger really is! It makes no sense to walk around a city like New York, amongst so many restaurants and eateries, with an empty stomach and a mind full of dread. A person should be able to walk up to any food vendor and ask politely for anything on the menu. Anything one wishes to eat should be given gratis.

Was that a good enough joke for ya? Have a hearty laugh at that one, friend, and don't worry, there'll be plenty more where that came from, I promise. A person tells you a story and you either listen or you don't but whatever conclusions you arrive at are your own. It's all fragments, never the whole truth.

If I ever get my hands on a substantial amount of money I'll feed this city block by block for free for days. There'll be signs posted all over town: *Hungry?*

*Show up to such-and-such a place at this time for a free meal and a few songs*. There'll be free medical checkups too. If we need to be disguised under the banner of some kind of a city government organization then so be it, for the authorities will surely get worried and wonder what the hell we're up to.

'We're not up to anything. Just doing God's work. What God? . . . Oh, whichever you say, mister.'

We won't talk to any reporters and will not allow any to infiltrate our ranks with their dirty mind/body/spirits. Our story will not be for sale either. Our deeds will live on in the hearts of women, children, and men. We'll require no publicity beyond word of mouth. TV newsmen? Ha! Please do us a favor and not even bother, we don't care about your opinions so leave us be. There'll be no dubious interviews while people wave to the cameras in the background. We'll only talk to those who understand. The rest can read our books and listen to our songs. Let them make up their own tales and spin them any which way they want to, with commercial breaks in between.

From us there will be no manifestos, no ten pillars of our cause, no constitutions, no commandments, no laws or codes of conduct. The atmosphere will be one of joy and peaceful harmony, a serene quiet harmony. Just words and melodies, transpicuous to some, yet utterly discordant to others.

The books are free if you've got reverence for the

moment, otherwise you've got to pay, pal! That's right, in cold hard cash too. Or you can give your shoes to that man over there, that's right, trade and barter like the days of yore. Who are we? Why, same as you, mister, we're human beings and we care for the well-being of our fellow human beings. We know, as surely you must too, that people are hungry both in their hearts and in their bellies. So we decided to take the easy way out and fill up their bellies. The rest will have to wait for now.

Oh how glorious it would be to feed thousands of people in the middle of this big bad city. To stop and divert the traffic like the NYPD does anytime there's some useless politician in town or a stale parade is commencing. Why not stop it to break bread? There'll be no bullhorns or loudspeakers, no yelling at the top of the lungs, and no electrified instruments of any kind for the many musicians. If you can't sing or play for small pockets of the crowd or verbalize necessary instructions without the aid of synthetic amplification then you do not work for us. May no harm come to you, friend, but we do not require your services. Feel free to stay and eat though. Yes, stay and enjoy yourself. The meals will of course be vegetarian, locally grown, and transported using bicycles.

Why not? It will be a tremendous undertaking. Let the rich and shameless have their banquets. This will be ours. Every crazy idea is welcomed by our staff, who will be handpicked by me and paid handsomely for their efforts. This won't just be food. This will be a bounty, a precious bounty, blessed by holy men and women. The cuisine shall reflect the multinational tastes of the city. Dozens of varied prayers will be said before we feast, but again not using bullhorns for there will be no bulls in sight, only us humans. It should be easy enough to accomplish, wouldn't you say?

*The road beckons adorned with jewels and precious alloys. The gunpowder is ready to spark and the cannonballs are stacked. Parakeets in the thousands, not caged but tied together with Invisi-string (GREAT NEW PRODUCT: Commercial says so), fly the colors of the visible spectrum. Can't fret about problems of city, country, world, or rent/ interpersonal. Demon button ready for the pressing. Monster time! Screw everything, man . . . Who cares?*

One of the upstairs neighbors is visiting us and talking about art. He used to be a big shot back in the nineties, came up with some way to exploit people in the digital age and got himself some notoriety. He housed people in a building and made sure all privacy was taken away from them. His ideas are all capitalist although he considers himself an artist.

'You see it's all about getting people to like your

troupe on this platform, if they like what you're wearing and your style and such. The goal is to get these people to come online anytime you say, then you can sell whatever you want to them, see. Let's say they like what you're wearing . . .'

He was blabbing on like that for a while and none of the kids or their manager had the balls to retort. I finally had to.

'I'm sorry, but what does that have to do with music?' I asked him.

'Well, music is part of it. You get these networks of people to come online anytime you want—'

'And you sell them things?'

'Yes, that's the goal.'

'As well as music?'

'Yes, they come because they relate to you, because they like what you're wearing, the music etc., they could be anywhere in the world! Advertisers and investors can easily see who has the biggest network and ah—'

'Right, but that's exactly what's wrong with everything. It's not about the quality of the music, is it?'

'Yes, it's a business!' he says, very irritated by my presence and attitude.

'It's all about that obituary in the *Times*, man, are you going to have a big one or none at all? That's what it's all about,' he says slyly, as a finishing blow.

'I don't give a shit about that. Did Van Gogh have a big obituary in the fucking *Times*? Is there nothing else to be done with these people once they like you but sell them something on behalf of advertisers? Can't we give them something?' I say.

The neighbor is fuming now and the manager tries to calm the situation and succeeds in doing so in his usual managerial manner.

Why don't we speak of Sumer or Elam? Well . . . okay, I don't really want to either. Girls? You wanna talk about girls? Okay. Let's do it. Why not? Let's get serious. 'Down to brass tacks' as the Americans say. Hey! I'm an American! Also an Iranian! A citizen of the world! Bring the beer, pills, and coke. Girls? Forget girls. Don't bring 'em near me. Don't wanna look at 'em. Don't need a girl, don't want a woman, don't care. That Plain Jane turned Ava Gardner turned on me. That wretched woman with a twisted heart. Lesson! Lesson! Learn! *Learn!*

I must have written five hundred pages. It sure did feel like it. I wrote and wrote and wrote for a couple of weeks straight after Josephine's . . . after Josephine, that cunt. She did not have to end it like that, that liar. Why lie? That weak little thing. Who is she, you ask?

Oh, forget it, she's nobody. Nobody to me anyway.

These Brooklyn streets are jam-packed with people. My boots need to be re-soled but when? I'm starting to look like Charlie Chaplin's Little Tramp. These here boots have been all over America thrice and once around England. My buddy Jake bought them in Hamburg and wore them all over Europe before giving them to me. Buy some cheap beer. Look at all these young girls in short shorts and tiny summer dresses strutting their stuff. Music pours out of many doors. Lots of bands playing live. Smell of food mixed in with foul body odor and perfume. Ah, forget it, keep moving, go back to the loft. The loft is full of people, a dinner party, right, I forgot. Food, wall projection, smoke, drink, conversation, funny clips, laughter, some girls I don't recognize.

'Hello.'

'Hello.'

'I'm Brittany.' Handshake.

'I'm Ali.'

'Nice to meet you.'

'You too.' What, where, when? Forget it, keep moving. It's all fun and games now, forget the heavy stuff. Oh, right . . . you wanted to talk about girls. Well, sorry, pal, guess I got a little carried away. Love? What love? What does any of it mean really? I don't care about definitions, don't want revelations and a whole lot of hullabaloo. It's all jagged and weird. Don't hurt me, mister . . . I don't want to hurt *you*, mister . . . What? You want to buy two cigarettes from me for a dollar? I only have three left, mister . . . How come? Don't ask me, mister, I'm clueless. The government don't run a thing by me. No decisions are made with my point of view in mind and it's probably a good thing.

She's speaking English in the room again – the journalist/writer/singer/wife/daughter/graduate/traveler. Her accent is interesting. There sure are a hell of a lot of us living and staying at this loft apartment. Some of these kids are younger than my younger brother. What happened? The dinner party is over? One of the young ones just fried some potatoes for us to eat with ketchup. I suggested dijon mustard and he agreed. Yummy, yum, yum. Good nutrition if you ask me. Fills you up, anyway. I just ate the second to last one and he ate the very last one. Good for him. He's young and needs his nourishment.

Maryam! Where are you? Hope you're well. Why didn't you take care of me? Me and you, baby! Me and you, we could have gone far together. Was it the sex? Yeah. I know it was . . . Sorry, I was young then, you know? Give it another try. Once more around the old block. Just once more for old times' sake. Your boyfriend? Oh, right . . . him. I love him . . . great guy, but . . . I really do love him, he's great, but . . . Pass the whiskey please. And the joint. I'll take one of those pills too, yeah, and a little hash. Food? Food. Food is good. You need food to live but not now.

*Lost in the sauce or wandering the spasmodic deserts of my thought streams, with the past a heavy weight that keeps the present and future in turbulent limbo.* What am I doing? I'm supposed to go on the road with these Iranian rock 'n' rollers again. It's a coast-to-coast tour and I figure the road is just as good a place as any to hide out for a while.

*Some of us it seems are destined to toil in the lonely desert of the awakened souls, where not even death provides relief or releases the choke hold. In this desert one wanders for an eternity alone and every encounter with another being is either imagined or real but the difference is indiscernible. All of the known laws, facts, lies, truths, questions, and answers flow through one's being at once, shooting out explosively at random intervals, and then the ground disappears before the endless floating through space begins. It is then that one awakens from one reality, to find new life in another, but since there is no way to tell or keep time in this desert the duration of these events is either equal to the time it takes to blink an eye or for a glacier to melt completely. Everything folds back onto itself.*

Couldn't find any Henry Miller for sale on my walk

past the street vendors yesterday. What? Not even in his Williamsburg, Brooklyn, neighborhood, not even in the old 14th ward? Or maybe the books fly off the shelf (table) in a flash as soon as they appear. No way to be sure.

Our travel plans seem very vague at this point or maybe I haven't been paying attention. We leave for Atlanta tomorrow. I have to buy some strings for my guitar but can't seem to leave this loft and I have little money. Everybody is always coming and going in this business. Timmy just flew to Amsterdam, Dariush is back from Prague, Gena just moved to Athens, and so on. The rest of us are about to scatter all over the country.

What will I do tonight? Don't want to go to any bars, don't want to see any people, don't want to sit here all night. New York, New York, a couple more days of being your crestfallen guest and then goodbye for a while.

New York is a state of mind. The best thing it can do for you, especially in America, is show that living like an artist is okay, or at least plausible. Living like an artist? What is an artist? I won't begin to try and define it, but will confess to knowing a little bit about the affair. Artists are considered crazy even by other so-called artists in this country. What a crime it is to be an artist in America.

It's a life lived near or below the poverty line, dotted with countless calamities of the spirit, suicidal tendencies, gross misunderstandings with other human beings regarding every aspect of existence. Not to mention cheap beer and whiskey, loneliness, pain, sickness, sorrow, mournfulness, compunction, malnutrition, cheap sex, booze, tears, regret, shame, guilt, vice, distress, misery, exultation, boasting, retreating, advancing, fucking, sucking, getting fucked, going broke all the time, always broke, sometimes a star, star for a night, promises, promises, machinery in motion, big wheels turning, potential, girls, money, sex, power, cool, rock 'n' roll, fantasy, dream come true, art galleries, paint, canvases, papers, pens, computers, drugs, booze, girls, guys, dudes, bitches, witches, whores, fuckers, drunks, druggies, yuppies, rich ones, poor ones, managers, agents, girls, girls, girls, light, dark, hair, clothes, guitars, drums, roadies, setting up your own gear, write a song, good song, bad song, shitty song, sells a million copies, YouTube hit, 'MTV doesn't play music videos anymore,' everybody plays music, music is big, art is big, entertainment is big! Biggest it's ever been, gigantic, huge, *huge*!

Just need to get away from that sort of thinking. Hope to slowly drift away from certain notions of self and existence. Too much noise in this loft now, the kids are watching YouTube, there is a neighbor eating one of the hamburgers they made, my mood is not an easy one, I am drunk and stoned, again. Nothing special to report here. If you want to know what's going on anywhere, if you want to know what the *deal* is anywhere in the world, then go there and stay a while. I wish I was going somewhere (Paris, London, Asunción, Tokyo, Arles, Casablanca, Nairobi, etc.) to stay for a while but instead my home will be where these crazy Iranian rock 'n' rollers take me for the next few months. God, Universe, Mother Earth, save us.

New York is where I started to write in earnest. In that Upper West Side apartment so tastefully decorated with imported vintage furniture and sculptures. Mana's gay old uncle who'd long ago moved to Tunisia had handpicked each piece and purchased them in places like Laos, Morocco, Nigeria, and so forth. Lots of paintings too and great big lively plants that gave life to the three-bedroom apartment. I put pen to paper immediately in that maid's room I slept in. How romantic it all was with jazz on the radio, that very first morning with the sun rising slowly above the old buildings. I didn't sleep a wink the first week in town, watched the sun come up every day, used to write on subways, in the park, on stoops, mostly songs back then but some prose as well.

It was a new world and wide open for me. I remember all those older Iranian artists that Mana's parents knew. Most of them had come over during the late seventies and early eighties. They did it right, dug in their roots and stayed put, some of them accumulated wealth and some came from money. There was the gay Assyrian poet and playwright who had a face like Hemingway and spoke the most velvety fine pomegranate-scented breezy English I'd ever heard, liked to call you 'dahling' and speak of Christ whenever possible. The Assyrian gay blade, with a crimson fiery soul like Ashurbanipal and a belly like Socrates. He used to be rich in the late seventies on account of his car blowing up and him winning the lawsuit.

'My more industrious friends advised me to invest my million or so in real estate. "Dahling, why don't you buy a building?" they asked. I was busy putting on plays and became at once disturbed by their vision of me as a person. My dissatisfaction was total. "What? Me?" I kept asking them in disbelief. "You must be joking. A landlord! I am an artist, dahling." Can you imagine me collecting rent from poor innocents? I would go bankrupt in a year!'

Of course he did go bankrupt and was working at Starbucks at the end of his life while living in a halfway home in the Bronx, but he kept putting on one-man shows that were the stuff of legend. He had a bewitching stage presence and a voice that seemed to come right out of the Delphic fissure.

There were a few filmmakers, many musicians,

painters, and writers too. We'd always spend the Fourth of July at one of their homes on Staten Island, right where the ferry docks and one can see the fireworks all over the city. They were a merry bunch and loved to drink as much as I did. A few master chefs hovered among them too, there was always a table adorned with the best dishes for all to enjoy.

Watching the exiles celebrate the Fourth of July was a strange experience because the duality in their emotions was nakedly exposed. They all longed for a homeland where they might be appreciated by their countrymen but instead were now growing old in a foreign land that guaranteed them freedom but little in the way of recognition. Their hearts still beat to distant memory drums of home.

They would still embrace, raise their glasses towards the fireworks, and sing merrily. At each other's funerals they'd read poetry. I was at a few of those funerals and sensed the exclusivity they clung on to. The torch was theirs to carry and none of us young folks were worthy of it. They were the generation that lost everything. Us, the young, didn't lose anything as far as they were concerned because we never earned anything in Iran.

On the other side of town, that Upper West Side apartment was saturated with the echoing voices and invocations of the old artists.

'And don't you know Lee J. Cobb was the best ever

in *Death of a Salesman*? And Tallulah Bankhead wanted to fuck Marlon Brando? Monty Clift killed in Lillian Hellman's *The Searching Wind* . . . and what about Paul Robeson's Othello? The best ever! Clifford Odets' *The Big Knife* . . .'

On and on up to the sixties now – 'Al Pacino in *The Indian Wants the Bronx*? Oh my God, genius, go up to the New York Public Library central branch and you can see it on video by request, genius, genius!'

In another room in between discussions of politics and sociology some talk of music – 'Have you heard Arthur Rubinstein's recording of Manuel de Falla's *The Fire Dance*? It'll change your life' – and some young guitar prodigy from Juilliard is playing a tune surrounded by wine-drinking people throwing shadows on the wall, 'Nobody can touch Yehudi Menuhin on violin . . . I love Toscanini! I don't understand John Cage . . .'

The shadows are dancing on the paneled walls of the living room. Down the hall people are laughing and smoking, the smoke curling up and more shadows, the paintings behind them taking on a different dimension against the honey-beige straw-cloth walls. A professor from NYU is lounging on graceful curvy furniture in another room, behind him some crimson velvet curtains and in front a marble column supporting a bleu-de-roi vase and candelabras and plates of fruit. He's talking about sex in the sixteenth century with an air of pugnacity.

It was all very normal somehow. And what about Rodgers and Hammerstein? Present. Ethel Merman? Also present. Eartha Kitt, Lester Young, Charlie Parker, Bette Davis, Marilyn, oh Marilyn! Everybody was there in speech and thought. Einstein and Rabelais, Nietzsche and Rumi, Maria Tallchief and Balanchine, Basquiat and Vermeer.

Some guy is telling another guy about the old Patagonian Express, another is cursing the Iranian regime, another the American regime. All swirls with magic and wine, spinning faster and faster day after day. From hollow viscera to somatic tissues, from deep and unknown to familiar, known, undeniable. Precambrian rock rising out of the earth in one room, in another mangroves and palms, azaleas, great crowned oaks, pawpaws, crape myrtles. People are standing on upland steppes and shouting at the ones walking around the deserts, pointing to forested mountains and pasture lands with grazing herds of cattle. I'm there with my vestibular impulses dead, not knowing whether I'm floating or standing on solid ground, and I'm saying to myself, Where are all the telephone booths, the long shiny Cadillacs, where are the typewriters? Is there any room left for artists in this saturated ghost town? My head aches and I'm dizzy again. I'm an immigrant awash in immigrant finalities, without sharp teeth with which to tear off a nice juicy piece of America's flesh for myself. American dreams bounce around my tired brain but don't stick to the gooey walls. Where are all the songs? Where is the poetry? It's different now and you know it. Change with the ever-changing times, my boy, and never fret, I repeat over and over with a glass of Scotch on the rocks in my hand.

But that was a long time ago. I've been to Niagara Falls since then and been hypnotized by the mystical deadly waters, I gave it a piece of my soul. I've scattered little pieces of my soul all over America, stashed them away in small towns so I can go and gather it back up if I ever needed to. Don't you know that the party never stops in New York? I'm sick of parties, you can't ever talk to anybody. I've been on the trains, the planes, the buses, the cars, what to do, what to do?

# The Tour

The tour was going well until we arrived in LA and everything went to shit. What's wrong with that godforsaken city? What compels people to behave in the manner they do there? The show was all right but the next few days were spent chasing tail and smoking opium, two things that don't go together at all. One can't really give two shits about anything on opium. Women and sex are still things one desires, but upon the slightest hint of failure the mind recoils and retreats back to its den of comfort and despair, provided there is opium waiting in that den.

I've given up on sex for the time being. It's too difficult when there are five other guys around at all times. Four horny musicians and one even hornier manager. Most of the time I have a chance with one of the best-looking girls around but somehow the opportunity gets squandered. I've lost the killer instinct. Some of the other guys are fucking-machines. Koli got laid by three different women in a forty-eight-hour period and still found time to smoke some opium in the interim. The first one he had was a rich widow with a gigantic house on the Hollywood Hills. She invited us over to her mansion where other available 'ladies' waited with delight and candor, the sort of fair-mindedness any rock 'n' roll musician looks for in the eyes of a woman or girl. I immediately locked in on a long-legged brown-haired siren who had, it soon became apparent, a ping pong fetish.

'Hit it hard! Harder! Make the ball hit me, come on! Can't you hit me?' she kept yelling. I could hit her but not in the way she really wanted to be hit. What can you do? She still seemed to like my company but after the cocaine arrived and I started to get into it, her friend kept pulling on her shirt and asking her to leave. One can always count on a good friend to screw it up for everybody. Siamak had a girl and so did Manuchehr, but the manager was in some kind of a stupor so we decided to drive to the beach and see the sunrise. On the drive my mind started to drift like it often does. For some reason I started to remember Amber. I met Amber on the highway a few years back – she was traveling with a friend.

My old pal Jake and I were on tour, driving across Kansas. We had just been pulled over and searched thoroughly by some dingbat cop with an SS hairdo and piercing Nazi eyes. The fucker could have found all sorts of goodies if he'd only looked hard enough, but what can you expect from a dumb Kraut pig? Needless to say we were not in the finest of moods, but suddenly a car pulled up next to us and after a moment Jake informed me that the occupants of this vehicle were two attractive females. I didn't care about any females, there'd been lots of them along the way: treacherous young witches, old sorcerers, students, mothers, girlfriends, daughters of the revolution, good-timing whores, sluts, broads, intelligent ingenues, wildcats, cougars, drunkards, closet lesbians, Midwestern midwives, nurses, lawyers, painters, assistants to Congressmen, strippers, pole-dancing specialists, bohemians, yuppies, yippies, hippies, honkies, hipsters, screamers, moaners, quiet types, skinny, voluptuous, blondes, brunettes, redheads. Not that we'd gotten our end in with them all, but close.

Thirty-six cities in forty-two days, opening up for an icon of sorts. Coast to coast, up and down, side to side rock 'n' roll fantasy. Intense madness that had mushroomed into something unmanageable by the end. We had crossed mountains, rivers, gorges, canyons, lightning storms, floods, bridges, ghost towns. Slept in five-star hotels, roach motels, strange apartments, on greasy linoleum floors, parquet floors, grass, gravel, dirt. We had become monsters, Jake and I.

All innocence was lost within us. We had morphed into politicians, pawnbrokers, pragmatists, hustlers, midnight ramblers, mutant methodologists grappling with the inescapable horrors of our free enterprise system, or so it seemed.

I decided to glance over and have a look and, low and behold, my steam-loving, dried-fish-eating, Swedish friend was right. These two were really something, a blonde and a brunette, probably from Scandinavian stock. A few more miles, a few more looks, then phone numbers were exchanged via the trusted big marker on paper trick. We decided to pull over at the nearest rest stop, which happened to be pretty far away and a Native American store. Once out of the car we all realized a connection had been made.

Amber was an amateur photographer and her friend Sara an amateur musician. They were coming from Las Vegas and on their way to Austin, where they planned to pack up all of their belongings and move to Los Angeles. Sara had spent the better part of the week fucking the shit out of some rich dude in Vegas, while Amber had watched and participated when the mood was right. Sara was a kind of S&M freak, I noticed, after she spotted a black leather whip at the Native American store and proceeded to whip me, rather hard, on the back and ass while laughing sadistically. There was nothing more Jake and I could do but to press on to the nearest motel and see about learning a trick or two from these wild vamps.

We hardly had any money, hadn't made any money from the past few shows, and were planning to sleep in the van but, what the hell, we just figured on not eating tomorrow. These girls were used to that rich guy in Vegas and we had to play up the cheap-motel, rough-sex factor to our advantage. They insisted on getting their own room and we were soon separated into couples. Once in the room I pulled out a half-full bottle of whiskey and a few Hydrocodone. The girls had a little coke and we did that at the natural entr'actes.

It wasn't so much the sex I was thinking about on this drive with the manager down to the beach but how easily I gave in to it. How easily I cheated, how easily I became a deceiver. It was a long time coming and once the floodgates opened there was no stopping the flow. A woman should always keep her man feeling manly or it just won't work. Men are stupid and should be treated like children most of the time. Amber made me feel like a man. She wasn't such an S&M freak after all, just a girl looking for a good lay in the middle of nowhere. After we were finished she lay there beside me and wanted to cuddle.

'Listen, Amber . . . I'd rather sleep in the other room, I'm gonna go check and see if they're done.'

'What? Why don't you sleep here?'

'Well . . . I'd be more ah—'

'You have a girlfriend, don't you?'

'Eh . . . yeah.'

'I knew it! Okay, I understand . . . I mean, yeah, all

right, but make sure you say goodbye before you guys leave, will you?'

We left the next morning bright and early without saying a damn word to them. Mana called from her job back in New York and we talked as if all was normal. Am I a monster? What is a monster? A liar, yes. A cheat, yes. A charlatan, yes. How did I manage to look my girlfriend in the eye and lie to her over and over again? I chalked it up to dissatisfaction and the law of keeping your guilt to yourself. I don't know. None of it was making sense anymore. I felt farther and farther away from having a meaningful relationship with a woman every day, thought it was truly the beginning of the end of the world.

I was hanging in the balance, somewhere between fantasy and reality. A fool completely engaged in self-destruction: a masochist, a contrarian, a liar, a cheat, a whore, a ghost, a shell, a dope fiend, pothead, cokehead, speed freak, pill popper, boozer, sex fiend, loner, alone. Artist?

I could feel the tide shifting during our New York shows on that tour when all the friends, record-label folks, PR folks, agents and managers had the look of fear in their eyes. What the hell has he been into? they all seemed to be thinking. Is this a joke? What is he doing? I didn't care about any of them anymore. Didn't care if they jumped in the East River or the Hudson. What did they know? Nothing, that's what. I hadn't been able to properly communicate with any of them for a while anyhow. We had such different tastes in everything. They all bathed in the river of commercialism and conformity.

Mana tried as best she could, I guess, to cheer me up, but that wasn't exactly her strong suit. We were disintegrating fast. That goddamned Brooklyn apartment of ours was beginning to feel like a tomb. The other tour I was supposed to go on went bye-bye and there I was, broke again. I spent the better part of the next six months chain-smoking, popping whatever pills I could get my hands on, and drinking heavily. I must have written and recorded some songs, gigged around town, and played a few festivals too, but the memories are rather hazy. I was mostly dying – slowly, yes, but dying nevertheless.

# Dallas

So right after that the relationship tanked and I was back in Dallas, hanging out with old friends, driving down the same haunted dead streets.

The Dallas/Fort Worth Metroplex, as they call it, was in my eyes a vast, soulless, decaying, hellish wasteland full of waterheads and dullards. After I escaped I would only come to town to see family, sometimes friends, and to play a show or two. (There is one place of refuge in D-town and that's my old buddy Jake's studio. A gear-head, analog freak's fantasy land; every old synthesizer you can name, organs, keys, etc.)

The very sight of the landscape could bring about a bout of nausea within me. 'Big D' was a link to the most lonesome death, a bridge to a place where dreams get crushed and recycled into shiny lies to be fed to the subjugated minions screaming for more. It is a hideous city built on commerce and power-mongering. One to be tolerated only a few days at a time and only out of obligation. Unfortunately it's also the home of my family, and I needed family at that time. Also, I needed a job.

'I can get you a job at this breakfast place,' my old high-school buddy Fernando says to me. With the amount of money he claims to make I wonder why he doesn't just peel a few bills off the top of his heap to get me by.

'Ah, man . . . the last thing I want to do is wait tables,' I say.

'I know, I know. Just until you find something else.'

'Yeah . . . I better, there isn't shit out there right now.'

'Okay, I'll talk to my friend. I'm pretty sure I can hook that up for you though, don't worry.'

Right, I won't worry. Why, old friend, can't we do something as men? We are men after all and this is America. Where is our pioneering spirit? To which he may rightfully answer, 'My pioneering spirit is just fine, buster, go make some money and then we'll talk.'

A couple of days later I get the job. Days blend into nights and back into days again. A few days later Fernando and I are at a local bar designed, built, and furnished for scholars of the art of obtuseness and he's talking.

'What is wrong with these girls? She seemed so interested, came up to me, gave me her number. I texted her and she answered back in like two seconds. Keeps saying, Let's go out, let's go out, and then . . . Look at this.' He shows me the text on his iPhone. It's very cold and standoffish. Says something like, 'Thanks for being nice but I don't think it's the right time for me.' 'What the hell does that mean? Right time for what? What the hell does she think, I want to marry her?'

'Man, didn't you say she just got divorced or something?'

'Yeah, but I don't know how long ago. Scared little girls, all of them. I just don't get it. I'd rather they don't give out their numbers at all. I don't wanna waste my time.'

'I know. Forget about it. This town . . . Man, I don't know,' I mumble back. I'm horny as hell myself and need the touch of a woman. There are a few attractive cocktail waitresses at this bar but they all seem to favor Fernando's style and grace. There will be nothing doing here.

Fernando doesn't get into drugs of any kind, the guy barely likes to take headache medicine, for Christ's sake. Much like all my other old high-school buddies he was now a successful businessman. Owned a house, an expensive car, was divorced, and had a couple of kids. I don't feel like staying here all night, don't like the people, don't like the music on the digital jukebox, the atmosphere reeks of TV commercials, but it's still too early to go home.

'What do you feel like doing?' I ask.

'I don't know, man, I'm kind of tired.'

'Yeah, bet you've got a crazy day tomorrow, ha?'

'Man, every day is crazy. It's my turn with the kids tomorrow too, on top of everything else.'

'Well, let's finish these beers and get the hell out of here,' I say, thinking he must still be tired from the night before. We had been sitting in a strip club on the slimy side of town, with drinks in front of us, waiting for his favorite girl to get off stage and dance for him. My favorite girl was rubbing her ass on some rich-looking older fellow who probably drove a twelve-cylinder Mercedes-Benz and owned land all over the great Republic of Texas. That special nudie-bar smell was in the air, the music was loud, and the lights were flashing green and red through the fake smoke from the stage.

I like to listen to strippers talk as much as I like watching them dance. They always want to tell me their life stories for some reason, and it's always the same old tale of abuse, teen pregnancy, self-preservation, single motherhood, drugs, booze, no hope, and how the fight or flight response is taking a heavy toll on their synapses. There are those few 'exotic dancers' who manage to get a higher education out of the deal, but those are rare cases. Of course all stories end with the inevitable 'You want a dance now or what?' line, but shit, the girls have to make money, that's why we are talking in the first place, and far be it from me to disrupt the free-enterprise system. I listen intently to their tall tales, offer some words of encouragement, and try to be a model customer.

I'm driving now, Fernando has gone home. I've already called my old drug buddy Joe and he's meeting me at a bar in the city of Addison, a suburb of Dallas. I'm walking in the bar now, it's one of the few places you can still smoke cigarettes in around these parts, and it reeks of it. Joe is standing at the bar.

'Hey, man!' he yells in my direction.

'What's up, Joey?' I yell back.

'Oh, nothing, man. Want a beer?'

'Yeah . . . have you made the call yet?'

'Yeah, drink the beer. It should time out perfectly.'

I work on the beer as I smoke a cigarette and look around the place. Same old tired faces, some lame chicks, dudes playing pool, a couple of attractive girls surrounded by a platoon of men, the jukebox is playing a Rolling Stones tune. We're in Joe's car now, he's playing me his new recording, it sounds good enough but the lyrics are hard to understand, we've smoked some weed out of his one-hitter, and we're driving across the street to meet the man who possesses the best stuff around these days. You call him, go inside the restaurant where he works, wait for him in the bathroom, and within a few minutes walk out with high-grade cocaine.

We drive to the back of the place where it's darker and do a couple of gigantic lines off a CD case. Feeling really good now and ready to drive downtown for action. Joe and I have become close lately. We are the same age, musicians, and both live with our parents. He never really did anything with music though, besides play around Dallas sporadically. For a decade he has been talking about moving to Germany, since he is a genuine Kraut on both sides of the family and has Kraut citizenship, but he just can't seem to take the final step.

We are not planning anything special tonight. It's just another normal night of cocaine, booze, and pills. Everything else is secondary. We pull up to our first destination, a dark and dungeon-like dive-bar on the backside of downtown, walk up to the bartender and order a few drinks.

'Give me some more,' I say to Joe, and he slips me the baggie he has hidden in the folds of a matchbook, and I go to the bathroom for a few bumps. The stuff needs to be crushed. The key I'm using is to my mother's Nissan. What the hell is happening to you? I ask my image in the bathroom mirror, then walk out.

Joe's talking to some girl, I leave him be, lean against the bar, and look around. My mind is racing and I'm wishing there was a piano I could play somewhere in the back. My sense organs are either flourishing or dead. My occipital lobe throbs. The thalamus region of my brain is quickly taking over while the left cerebral hemisphere tries desperately to maintain control. Will conflict and confusion prevail tonight? I think, as my mind drifts towards images of the Great Smoky Mountains and the Allegheny River for some strange reason. I feel the sudden need to jump in a stream and purify myself. A friend told me about the Devil's River once. He spoke of how pristine the waters are, 'Clear as a swimming pool,' he'd said. The hollow center of my spinal column starts to itch but I know how impossible it is to scratch that region. My autonomic nervous system seems to be functioning fine, however. Some chemical compound is secreting from my nerve endings, digestive-system activity has been slowed, rate of respiration and heartbeat have been naturally accelerated.

'What's your name?'

'What?' I ask in the direction of the voice.

'What was your name again?' It is a female voice, coming from my left.

'My name? It's Amon.'

'Amon? Is it really?'

'Yeah, well, I'm a sinner, that's for sure. What's yours?'

'Stephanie.'

'Wow, what a beautiful name.'

'Really? You think so?' she says sarcastically.

'Yeah!'

'Don't you remember me, Ali?'

'Sure, Stephanie from a moment ago.'

'No, crazy. Jake's friend. We met last year when you guys were on tour? At the House of Blues?'

'Oh, right . . . Didn't we sing "The Battle Hymn of the Republic" together?'

'Never in hell, I don't sing Yankee songs, can't you hear my accent?'

'Sure . . . Well, whatcha drinkin', girl?'

'Beer, I've got one right now though. What are you doing here? Are you playing a show?'

'Yeah, and it's a long one too. It's this piece I've been working on. It's called "Days Run Into Nights and Back Into Days Again."'

'Oh, I see, how modern. Maybe you can turn them into months and years for Part Two,' she says, staring ahead.

'Wow! You really understand me, Stephanie! Wanna be my manager?'

'No, I don't deal with musicians like that.'

'Oh, fuck that shit, girl! We're gonna go right to the top me and you! Right to the top, I tell ya!'

'Okay, fine. How about a shot to celebrate?'

'Mighty fine idea, my dear lady. I don't drink fruity shit though. How about some whiskey?'

'How about it?' she says as she motions to the bartender with her head. The man behind the bar seems to know the score and quickly pours us a couple of shots. She doesn't even pretend to reach inside her purse to pay.

'Here's to something or other,' I say, we click our shot glasses together, and drink the cheap whiskey down. I start to recall how I came to meet Stephanie. She's always around this part of town. Jake has told me stories about her. She was a beautiful girl once. Got into Meth a couple of years back and disappeared for a while. God only knows what she's into now. Mostly hangs around dirty little bars and gets drinks bought for her, I guess. She still looks ravishing in dimly lit caves such as this when your head is getting screwed on tight with booze and coke.

'What are you guys up to tonight?' she asks.

'Oh, nothing much. Just killing time.'

'Oh yeah? What else?'

'You know what else. What, you want some?'

'Sure, whatcha got?'

'Let's go out back and I'll show you.'

She leads the way through the kitchen and out to the empty back patio. I give her a bump. 'Here you go, girl. Enjoy yourself.'

She snorts it. I give her another.

'And now the other nostril,' I say.

'Thanks, baby. How do I look?'

'Alluring.'

'No, my nose,' she asks.

'Oh, let me see . . . Clear.'

I do a couple of bumps then we go back inside. Joe comes up and wants the baggie. I sit down at the bar. Stephanie goes somewhere else and I silently wish her the best. I start to hear some song lyrics in my head and wish I still carried around a pad and pen. The rest of the evening unfolds in the same stolid fashion, follows the same pattern, and goes absolutely nowhere. A couple of more bars visited, a few more conversations, more drugs and booze. While driving back a cop car going the opposite direction pulls a sudden U-turn and follows us for a few miles. It's scaring Joe to death.

'Jesus Christ, the bastard's right on our ass. Fuck, he knows where we're coming from. Knows I'm drunk,' he says, glancing back and forth from the rear-view mirror to the road.

'Fuck him, just drive straight, a couple of miles over the limit, and get to the highway. What did you do with the coke?'

'Threw it under the seat.'

'Okay, just relax. We're not doing anything wrong. Well, not really.'

These goddamn cops around Dallas love to drive behind you and see if you swerve even a little. Gives them some kind of cheap thrill. If he pulled us over now we'd be in major trouble. They don't mess around in Texas. It's not like New York, where swerving and sudden speed changes are a normal part of everyday driving. In this town you better drive like a grandmother, especially if you're a dope fiend.

We finally make it to the main highway and lose the cop. Joe drops me off at my mother's car and says goodnight in his usual distant Germanic manner. I get behind the wheel, start to drive, and try to keep the car as straight as possible. It's so strange to be driving down these same streets again. Real time travel is when you are in the same places you've once been. *That's where June and I first kissed. That used to be her mother's house.* Ghosts of the past everywhere you look, phantoms of your memories around every turn. Am I the revenant? My mind is clear somehow. I feel as if I can see inside every home that passes and study the inhabitants' faces. House after suburban house full of sleeping souls dreaming of security, power, love, nightmarish scenarios, money, threesomes with teens, ball games, big raises, promotions, cheating, bigger pools, faster cars, God, monsters, TV shows, commercials . . . Not a safehouse in sight. I come to the grim realization that even if I ever in actuality find a safehouse, I will need a far longer stay than will be allowed me by the host.

Somewhere in the back of a neighborhood I pass through, inside a dark house, in the corner of a newly remodeled kitchen, sits a man staring out of his window. He is leaning on the table with his head resting on one hand. His wife and child are asleep on a king-size bed in the master bedroom. The full moon is unnaturally bright and reflects off of the chrome-plated pistol in his hand. He gets up slowly and walks to the master bedroom. The place looks like a page out of an expensive furniture store catalog. He looks at his sleeping family. His wife is losing weight on account of the new diet she's trying out. His daughter will be five years old in a week and is already diagnosed with six kinds of illnesses for which she takes seven different medications. I don't have a reason, he thinks to himself. I just want to, that's all. With that final thought he walks into the master bathroom and locks the door. The bathroom is finally looking exactly the way his wife had always wanted it to. The dream house will be quiet for a few more minutes before a loud gunshot awakens the man's wife and daughter.

Somehow I woke up the next day, dressed myself, and drove to work. I am a server, a servant, really. I take orders for a living. Deliver fat and grease to these elephants, these overweight slobs stuffing their faces. Pour coffee and refill their sodas. I am a zookeeper and it's feeding time for the animals. Every goddamned morning bright and early before day even breaks these hippos are knocking on the door. 'Good morning!'

What's so good about it, fuck face? I've been working here a month now. I had vowed never to wait tables again and that was when I worked at the restaurant overlooking the Van Nuys airport ten years ago. The fat slobs that showed up to weekend brunches there were really something to behold.

I tried getting some kind of an administrative job but in this damn recession you need an MBA to work as a toilet cleaner. This one place hired me a couple of weeks back for nine bucks an hour but there was a drug test requirement. I showed up to the testing center, which reminded me of the shittiest check-cashing place, in the shittiest part of the South Bronx, and went to the back for the test. While I was standing there holding my prick over the little plastic container something snapped inside. What the hell was I doing there? I thought. These rednecks were making me piss in plastic, for what? I walked out of the bathroom and threw the container in the trash while walking out.

'Sir? Sir! Where are you going?' the young man wearing latex gloves and waiting to receive and archive my piss asked me.

'I'm going to my friend's house to get stoned. You should come. Forget about these swine. You have no future here. Your whole life revolves around urine, for Christ's sake! Run for the hills, man!'

The poor bastard gave me a look reserved for mental patients but I didn't care. I was free. Or I was free until reality stuck a finger in my ass and reminded me to check my pockets and count the jingle-jangling change.

So now The Intercontinental Interplanetary Multi-denominational Pancake Agency is where I work. Yes, sir! I am a server. I am very professional and accommodating but you won't catch me bending down like some of my co-workers, or making buddy buddies with the animals. I am good-natured, hospitable, kind, courteous, polite, and all that stuff, but fuck you if you want anything more out of me. They don't pay me enough to entertain you folks, I used to make a grand a night playing shows, so go shit in a creek or whatever it is you yokels do around here. Don't get me wrong . . . I don't have anything against you, hell, you folks seem like good Christians. I can tell since you all bowed your head and prayed before you began stuffing your faces and have been smiling at me an awful lot, but for the love of Zeus just leave me be. Don't ask me any questions or my name. My name is Who-gives-a-shit, well, that's the English translation. It's translated from Hokan Indian. Native American, yes. My name is Hokan but I'm a Tonkawa. Hell no, I ain't a Mexican. If I take off this ugly uniform, the useless apron, and these polyester pants you'd see my tattooed body. My breechclouts might sexually arouse your teenage daughter a little too much for her own good. How old is she anyway? Ah, forget it, mister, I'll stick to your wife for now. Notice the way she's been looking at me? I think she wants to stick my entire body inside of her. Sorry, pardner, I'm a raider and a marauder and can't help myself. They've got me in this get-up and it itches. They tell me to take orders from you and then execute those orders. Can I go now? Have you had enough of talking to me?

It's a hell of a busy restaurant. I never knew so many people ate breakfast outside of their homes. There is a two-hour wait from 8 a.m. to 2 p.m. on weekends. It's a never-ending parade of hungry Harrisons, Carters, Johnsons, Patels, Rodriguezes, Tangs, Wangs, Nehi Nehi Kerdahes, Hushmanzadehs, Allah O' Akbar O' laho Akbars and the rest of the goddamned phone book. Why me, Lord? What lesson are you teaching me now? Don't you know I'm stupid and don't learn lessons? Can't you just give up on me and let me be rich and famous already? My first table on my first day was sitting at a booth above which hangs a big framed picture of the Empire State Building. That was some sweet and sour irony for me to feast on and made me chuckle with defeat.

Coffee, cream, water, put the order in the computer, 1 bac & egg, 2 eggs over medium, 2 sausages & egg, 2 eggs & 1 egg over easy, two white toasts, one sourdough, don't forget to drop the toast, go refill the coffee, new table, 2 OJs, 1 Cranberry juice, 2 kids' milks. 'Oh, right, hello! Good morning, yes.' Another table, 'Hello . . .' Hot tea. 'Damn you!' Get the tea set up. Lemon. 'Where is the lemon? Out of lemon already? Come on, people, who opened today?' Butter the toast, get strawberry preserves. 'José! *Dos papas, por favor! Sí, gracias*. Primo! Omelette ready? No? *Por qué? Trabajando?* Okay. No, no problem.' Holy screaming Jesus! I've only been here an hour.

On and on like that until I come home and wash the grease out of my hair and pores before taking a nap. If I'm lucky there are no waiter nightmares and I can wake up refreshed and enjoy the rest of my day. Most of the time I can completely forget about it. My friends and family know not to ask me about work. Work is work. Who wants to talk about work? Don't remind me! After my nap is when some normalcy returns. I'll usually eat an orange with some dried pumpkin seeds and try to replenish my reserves. I try to remember and remind myself of my aim in life. It's just a temporary condition, I think, one that will come to pass. It is not a hallucination but completely real. You are strong enough to handle it and come out with your pride and self-respect intact. After you wake up a bit go and play your guitar. Sing and be merry.

That night I get a call from Fernando. He says Josephine is in town and asks if I want to go to dinner with the two of them.

'What? Josephine, really?'

'Yeah. Do you want to go or what?'

'Of course! Pick me up will you?'

Fernando drives us downtown and I'm asking, 'So Josephine is back from Morocco. How did that happen?'

'She broke up with her Moroccan fiancé, went to visit one of her rich admirers in France, one thing led to another and here she is now. Will be leaving for Switzerland in a couple of days.'

Switzerland? Jesus, who is it this time? I wonder. 'And she always calls you when she's back, eh? What do you have going on with her? Isn't she basically responsible for your divorce?' I ask bluntly.

'She doesn't think so and neither do I. Jessica is another story,' he says in his cool and casual manner. 'What about you? Are you still crazy about her?'

I wouldn't know until I saw her face. Around five years ago Fernando and his then wife Jessica were having a party at some bar, I was in town and joined them. Josephine worked for Fernando at the time. One look at her and I knew she was trouble, a real seductress with entrancing eyes and a hypnotic voice. I was with Mana and tried to stay away but that just made her want to destroy my defenses. Not much came of it then or after because her and Fernando had something on the side. She was an aspiring writer and sent me some samples over the years. She also loved one of my songs so we kept in touch. I once tried to force myself on her but she wouldn't have any of it.

'You have shitty taste in men,' I mumbled at Josephine in Fernando's car after our dinner. 'You need an artist.'

'How do you know what I need? I've dated artists before. I don't ever want to date another artist again,' Josephine said from the front passenger seat.

'Oh, you've dated an artist, eh? Who? What kind of an artist? Was he ready to die in the gutter?'

'What are you talking about?'

'Well, what did he do? Was he a painter? Was he—'

'Painter, yes!'

'Okay, so what's wrong with that? You always pick these . . . I don't know. Don't you want to jump into the fire? I mean—'

'Fire? No, I don't need to jump into any more fires,

Ali. Why do you assume I do? Who's the right kind of man for me? You? Are you what I need?'

'No, that's not what I'm saying. You just . . . these men you keep talking about, they just aren't the right type for you. You're Josephine, goddamnit!'

'What does that mean?' she asked, laughing.

'You're special. You need a guy who's worthy of it. A guy who can handle the places you're going and who you'll become.'

I suddenly realized how drunk I really was and decided to stop flapping my jaws but didn't feel sorry about our little conversation. Fernando had remained silent throughout. He pulled up to her place to let her out.

'Thanks, guys, I had a great time. I'll see you in a few weeks. Bye, Fernando. Bye, Ali, try not to drink so much. It's not good for you.'

We said goodbye and watched her wait for the elevator, then wave and get in. She looked breathtakingly stunning that night. If only Fellini were still alive to see her. Fernando stayed silent.

'That poor girl. Every man she comes across wants to own her.'

'She knows what she's doing,' said Fernando.

A couple of weeks later I get a text from Josephine saying she's back from Switzerland and wants to hang out. I pick her up at her apartment. 'Will you give me a great big hug when you see me?' is another thing her text had read. The elevator door opens and she walks out looking beautiful. I jump out of the car and after saying hello embrace and squeeze her for a few moments. We get in and drive off. My aim is to be as cool as possible, charming, delightful, pleasant, engaging, and fun. I love her red lipstick, and the way she makes her eyes up is the stuff of movie magic. She seems to be lit in the right way at all times and the lighting has a film noir quality about it. Her voice and inflection are very sultry. She can modulate and change accents at will and is a master of pitch contouring.

We are conversing with ease and feel comfortable. Obviously something critical has come to pass on her travels. She's had to take decisive actions and evasive maneuvers. Some prominent and powerful individual has propositioned her in some way, tried to dominate and command her with enticing offers and promises of security. Her will and self-respect seem to have remained supremely intact but the episode has left her somewhat drained. I listen as if each word and sentence is of paramount importance. There isn't anywhere else in the world's past, present, or future I would rather be but right next to her in this car at this very moment. We arrive at the restaurant.

'I guess I can valet,' I say.

'Don't worry about it. It's a nice night. I could use the walk.'

I find a parking spot some place nearby and we start to walk. It really is one of those perfect Dallas nights, cool with a gentle breeze blowing. Once inside everyone from the host to the wait staff to the other diners looks at us. We order two glasses of red wine and settle back. The conversation is flowing again. The burning candle on the table is giving the right side of her face a perfect fluttering light, the backlight is provided by a soft overhead above the bar, the rest is perfect shadow play.

She speaks of the marvels and magical qualities of the French and Swiss Alps, and I listen intently. Once again my intention is to remain calm and composed, serene and tranquil. I'm trying to be worthy of the moment, have waited years for this and will not allow a lapse of some kind to ruin it. The conversation turns to our past as we reminisce about meeting each other years before and how I tried to get her to kiss me that one time in the hallway after a concert.

'God, your aura was so messed up . . . you were not in the right place,' she says.

'I know, what can I say? I thought about you so much after that.'

'Really?' She looks a bit surprised.

'Of course, thought about you all the time.'

'What did you think about?'

'About how much I wanted to have some time alone with you. Just a day or one night. I just knew that if we could have one uninterrupted night alone . . .'

'Yeah? What?'

'I don't know . . . that there could be a connection.'

'But we've always had a connection,' she says.

'Yeah . . .' I say, looking into her eyes and smiling.

The food comes and we start to eat. There is a guy/girl guitar duo playing Burt Bacharach covers in the corner, the table next to us is singing 'Happy Birthday' to one of the women as cameras flash and hugs and kisses fly. We order a couple more glasses of wine. Josephine is not sailing the calmest waters of her young life. Her eyes reveal much pain and sadness. Some deep desire has been sullied. A painful lesson has been learned. She talks about her mother for a little while and how much she misses her. Her mother died years ago, her father too, and she could sure as hell use some family right now.

'It's hard when you get offered everything you could ever dream of,' she says. 'Complete security, you know? But you aren't free anymore. If I took what was offered me I'd be walking into a kind of prison.'

I listen, nod, and respond but what the hell do I know? She's playing in another league. What would I do if someone offered me complete security? Frankly, I am surprised she didn't accept the offer. She's turned down many men in the past, to be sure. What is she looking for? Love? It means a lot to me that she's strong and independent. I would sit here for a million years and listen to her stories. Right here in this chair I would plant myself and gaze across the table at her until the end of time. We finish our dinner. I've barely eaten a thing, just a few bites. Who needs food? I wish I could take Josephine's hand and run away with her.

'Where do you want to go?' I ask while we stroll back to the car.

'Ah . . . Lae's at Seline Bar.'

'Okay, great. Let's go.'

Lae is her roommate and best friend. He is barely twenty-one and gay. I like him. We go to Seline Bar, order drinks, and chain-smoke on the patio. Josephine is loosening up now. She's being flirtatious. Lae is playing with my hair.

'I love your hair. Don't you just love his hair, Mama? It's so curly. I just wanna play with it,' says Lae.

'I know! One of these days I'll be pulling on your hair while you're inside of me,' Josephine says to me.

'Oh, yeah . . .' I say back, trying to act cool.

'I had a dirty dream about you last night,' she says.

'Really? What was it about?'

'Oh . . . it was dirty. You had your hand down my pants.'

'Hmm . . .'

'Yeah, it was steamy.'

'Well, I can do that for you if you'd like,' I say, looking into her eyes. 'Anytime you want.'

I have a powerful desire to rip her clothes off right there.

The drive back to her apartment seems to go by quickly. We sit in the car for a while and talk. Her phone keeps ringing. It's probably her boyfriend/ex-boyfriend. I don't know much of the story and don't really care. If it's the same Arab as before, which I suspect it is, then damn him, he's had his day.

'We've been sitting here a while. We could have gone inside,' I say.

'I can't show you my apartment. It's messy.'

'I like messy,' I plead.

'Why don't you drive up a couple more levels in the garage. It'll be more private,' she says.

I drive up a few more levels. Her phone keeps ringing. She picks it up.

'What! I am out . . . With a friend . . . I'll call you tomorrow . . . Look, I gotta go.' She hangs up. 'I'm sorry,' she says and turns off her phone.

'Don't worry about it. Is everything okay?'

'Yeah . . . no . . . My life has been so insane the last few months. I just need it to slow down a little. Only a little bit so I can find my balance again.'

'Sounds like it.'

She's staring at me with those eyes once more. Those eyes can make a man do anything. I will become an assassin if need be, an Apache warrior, an invader, a gladiator who has no choice but to stab his best friend through the heart.

'God, Josephine . . .' I sigh.

'What?'

'Do you have to look at me like that?'

'Like what?'

'You know like what.'

'I should just rape you right here in the car,' she says.

'No . . .' I say while leaning closer. 'Not here . . . not like this.'

'You want it to be special? You should get it while you can.'

'You're probably right . . .' I lean in real close now while looking deep into her eyes. It's time for something more. I glance from her eyes down to her lips.

'Do you know what kind of men fuck me, Ali?' she says, swelling with sex.

'What kind?'

'The kind that can take me and fill me up,' she says, kissing me for a moment then grabbing and squeezing my face.

'Oh, yeah?'

'Yeah, but do you know who else I fuck sometimes? Rarely, to be sure, but sometimes?'

'Who?'

'Little romantic types like you . . . good guys, the

kind who don't have it in them to throw me around or puncture me.' While she's talking she unbuckles my belt and unbuttons my jeans.

'It would take you ten thousand years to fuck me the way I want you to, you're too nice, but I like you, I've always liked you and I want you to get what you've been fantasizing about all these years. I want you to feel me inside.'

She's on top of me now with her skirt hiked up, before I know it I'm inside of her and she's riding me out of my mind. I am floating among astral plains. She is doing some kind of shape-shifting act, her jet-black hair morphs from one color to another. Her light brown eyes keep turning purple and red.

'Oh, Ali . . . don't you know who I am? Don't you remember me?'

'I know who you are.'

'No . . . you don't remember me.'

'What are you talking about?' I say, almost dying from pleasure.

'We've been together before, in past lives, I know of at least twelve other ones. I shouldn't be doing this with you but I can't help myself. It always ends the same way,' she whispers and moans while rocking up and down faster and faster. 'It can never be . . . right,' she keeps saying while moving up and down on my manhood. There is no way to hold it back.

'Josephine, I'm about to . . . slow down a little . . .'

'It can't ever be right,' she keeps saying.

'Josephine, I'm about to come, you're killing me.' I try to slow her down but she's in a world of her own. 'Josephine, you have to stop . . . get off or I'm coming inside of you.'

For some reason she's not listening to me and I can't throw her off. After it's done I feel like there is no life left in me. She grabs my face, kisses me on the lips, gets out of the car and walks to the elevator.

# New York

The rain was falling hard as I exited the subway station on 42nd St. and 7th Ave. to walk south. My shoes and socks were already wet from before and my black jeans were also on their way to being badly soaked. There was no time to get cleaned up before the job interview so I quickened my pace and tried to keep as dry as possible under the awnings. I really needed this job. Needed it badly. The ten dollars and thirty-seven cents in my left pocket had to be saved for transportation costs if I ever got the job. But what about the rest of it? Food, drink, cigarettes? What's the use of thinking of those things now, I thought, just before side-stepping a tall young brunette walking in front of me and hopping over a puddle in the middle of the street. My balance was slightly off as I landed and I reminded myself not to make any more sudden movements since I still had not fully recovered from another one of my lost weekends.

This billionaire had taken us out to a fancy bar/restaurant on Saturday night and spent six hundred dollars on us. He just 'loved' my voice, thought I could sing operatically with a little training.

'I want you to come over and let me coach you a bit. We'll start with you lying on the floor and breathing.'

'Come again?' I asked, almost choking on my drink.

'You'll be lying on the floor and I'll be examining your breathing.' He claimed to have studied opera before becoming a high-end insurance salesman.

'Breathing?' I asked.

'Yes, you just breathe and I'll observe you,' he said with a wine glass raised to his mouth.

'Aha, of course,' I said while glancing at Mary, who was trying to keep a straight face.

The man was a fruitcake and I was only there for the free meal and booze at Mary's behest. He'd told her how much he liked our music after seeing us perform one night and wanted to see how he could help. Of course he was also trying to get it on with Mary's friend Alberto, who was young and beautiful. Alberto was supposedly keeping the old-man billionaire on ice for us by playing hard to get.

Having been around the block a bit I've come to understand what these rich folks mean by helping, and it has nothing to do with giving you any amount of money, not in my case anyway, they're just bored and need something to do. There was no way I was going to sprawl out on this guy's floor and let him stick his thumb in my ass or whatever the hell he had planned in his head, but I was going to drink all the free absinthe he was buying. Mary had tried to seduce me again too of course, and man was it getting hard to refuse her advances.

'I wanted us to have an artistic relationship. I respect you so much as a writer, a painter, eh . . . I love your music . . . you love mine. Can't we just be friends? I'd really like to just be friends,' I'd told her a few times, to no avail.

'I'm falling for you, Ali,' she'd say.

My whole life I've tried in vain to be friends with female artists. When you want them to fuck you they seldom do, and when you want to be friends it's mostly impossible. The situation made me understand how women feel when a man is obsessed sexually and emotionally. I'd always understood that though, come to think of it, and didn't need a reminder. I just wanted to play music with her, to read her writing, and have her read mine, to have her help me with it. Her music was incredible, I thought, she loved mine, and we sounded even better together. I wanted to explore her art not her vagina, but she'd have none of it.

We met a couple of months ago when the kids and I were walking past my friend Laura's apartment to see if we could get some free weed from her. I tried to be friends with Mary and resisted her until finally she brought over some whiskey one night and cornered me on the rooftop. I caved in after half a bottle and the next thing I knew she was bringing me coffee wearing a kimono the next morning. But hell, it's New York and we were both single. What's a romp in the sack on a drunken night?

I'm in the elevator and up to the job interview in a flash.

'Good morning,' I say to the lady at the front desk.

'Hi, may I help you?'

'Yes, I'm here to see Isaac.'

'Okay, have a seat. There's a bathroom in the back if you want to dry off.'

I take her up on the offer. Oh, the garment district. How it's always held a nostalgic kind of fascination for me. I am an immigrant after all.

'Ali?' calls a tall, handsome, and very fit middle-aged man.

'Yes. Hello,' I say with a broad all American smile.

'Hi, I'm Isaac, come on back. So Jacob told me you're looking to work on the cataloging project.'

'Yes, I'd love to, sounds very interesting.'

'Oh, I don't know how interesting it is, but it has to be done nevertheless. So you guys met at the meditation camp, I hear?' he says, sizing me up to see if I'm a transient freak.

'Ha, yeah. Have you been?'

'Me? No, no. Jacob's tried to get me to go a few times but, ah, too busy, you know?'

'Of course.' I want to tell him I only went because of free meals, room, and board but restrain myself.

He explains that he wants me to photograph fabric samples for their website. 'Yeah, so it's twelve dollars an hour for the first week, let's do ten an hour to make sure we're on the same page and then twelve. I'll pay you cash. You can work up to let's say twenty-five, thirty hours. Okay?'

'Okay, great. Sounds wonderful, thanks, thanks very much.'

'No problem. Tomorrow then?'

'Of course, sounds great. See you then.'

I give him a manly handshake, walk out of the fabric store, and thank my lucky stars. Without this job I might as well start hooking. It's a change of pace too. Fabrics, designers, tailors, fashion crazies. I like being around fabrics, reminds me of my grandfather, who was a tailor. The smell of fabrics takes me back to the good old days of sitting by his side while he listened to his little portable radio back in Tehran. I only knew him as a retired man in his late seventies but he was a mystic who owned a garment factory and had known financial success for a time.

# Tehran

Grandpa had been a fair employer by all accounts but somehow or other had lost his business, and my grandmother supposedly supported the family for years through dressmaking at home. She was still at it when I was young and I remember her many sewing machines. She seemed to own one from every era. My favorite was an old treadle machine that looked to be a hundred years old. What a marvelous-looking thing that was: sleek, black, mysterious, dangerous. Anyhow the reason my grandfather lost his thriving business was never made clear to me and I was too young and respectful of my elders to ask him personally, but I was able to gather bits and pieces of the story. It all had something to do with his generosity and lack of education. Supposedly he'd shared an overwhelming amount of the company's profits with his employees as well as giving out loans left and right with no desire for repayment. Any request for a loan or handout was answered with an affirmative response without a second thought.

'Mister Garakani sir, my wife is ill and—'

'What? Your wife? Say no more, call Doctor Farzad and tell him to charge it to me.'

'Mister Garakani, my son, he's old enough to start school now and well . . . you know with the other kids enrolled we just can't . . . eh—'

'What are you hemming and hawing for, Gholam Reza? You need money for school books? Here. What are you beating around the bush for? I'm a busy man by God, can't you see I'm busy? Get back to work, here take some more money, don't waste my time, just come right out with it.'

'Thank you, God bless you, sir. Also, Mister Garakani, sir . . . my brother needs a job and—'

'Didn't I give your brother a job last week? Where is he anyhow?'

'No, sir, not Akbar. He's working upstairs, God bless you for hiring him. I'm speaking now of Asghar, who just got to town, he's a good worker.'

'Ah, I see, Asghar, why didn't you say so . . . well, bring him by and I'll talk to him.'

'He's right outside, sir, sitting under a tree.'

'Gholam Reza! Didn't I tell you I'm busy? Why are you keeping him waiting out there in the heat? Go get him so we can get it over with. *Astakhforela!*'

It must have been a never-ending procession of people asking for this and that because in those days people had an average of six or seven children, with three or four miscarriages and a couple of infant deaths on top of that.

Once he took me to the old quarter of Tehran, where the alleyways are too small for cars, to eat a traditional Iranian breakfast of guts and face meat, before going to Friday prayers, and everybody in the whole district seemed to know him. He was greeted like a high official. Anyway, the other contributing factor to the loss of the factory must have been his illiteracy. He'd told me the story when I was about eight years old, you'd never know he was illiterate from the way he spoke.

'Come here, son, sit here beside me in the sunlight.' He loved to sit on the floor under an open window with the sun shining through. 'You see my mother died when I was five and a couple of years later my father became deathly ill and knew the end was near, so he gathered all the money he had in the world and sold all that was of value then took the sum to his brothers, my uncles, and told them to put it towards my schooling. After he died I kept waiting to get enrolled in class. One year passed and I saw all the kids going to school. I was sent to work in a factory, another year passed and still nothing so finally I went to my uncles and asked them, "When am I going to school?" "School?" they said. "We don't have money for your schooling, we've taken you in and given you a job but we have children of our own and can't afford to pay for another child's education." I said, "But my father told me he'd left money for my education." My uncles said there was no such money and that my father had lied to make me feel at ease. All the while my cousins kept going to school as I worked in the factory. I'm not telling you this so you can feel sorry for me, you see, I want you to understand how important an education really is. Do you understand, son?'

I remember the anger I felt. Where were these uncles now? Dead to be sure, but where were they buried, these monsters? I had a few graves to piss on. Where were these cousins? Why would anyone do such a thing? Or did his father really lie about the money? That story was only one of the first to explain man's cruelty, there'd be many more coming my way, and at warp speed. The Iran–Iraq war was in full swing and would eventually leave half a million dead on each side. The government's prisons were overflowing with political prisoners, and the firing squads must have worked around the clock to keep up with the task at hand. Savagery and ruthlessness permeated every level of life as we knew it, the scale was biblical. The sadistic hand of man's obsession with power was ever present but what happened in Iran was not at all unique.

A lot of my contemporaries have witnessed the same things but have chosen to forget. I can't forget and can't self-medicate enough, and not even a lobotomy will suffice.

My grandfather's mother was said to be almost saintlike. She would give anything she could to those in need. She had a thing of giving her coats to a half-frozen passerby on the street, in the dead of winter. One of my grandmothers, my father's mother, was orphaned and married off at the age of eleven. She was clutching her little doll when they brought her by. She had her first child at fourteen. They were poor but no one can recall anything but a positive attitude from her. She died of a misdiagnosed heart attack after a visit to my imprisoned uncle. She was only in her early fifties. She used to always smile and say, 'It's all right, dear, everything's going to be all right. Everything's going to be just all right.'

The last time I saw my grandfather was in Germany on a visit. The Alzheimer's was eating away at his brain fast and he kept saying how much he loved Europe. 'I should have come here as a young man,' he kept saying. I found it hard to sit by his side then, just couldn't bear it. The old man died a few months later just before dawn back in Tehran. He still comes to me every once in a while in dreams to teach me things about life. He is my connection to my ancestral past, the deep past before the written word, before the Magi, before the kings, when men and women lived a harsh life among the living soil and watched the night sky for clues, before the fall, before the flood, before the hordes, in the open, together.

# San Francisco

We've got a show tonight at a big-time venue, opening up for some popular group out of San Francisco, for almost no money, of course. I play first, then the kids, then the popular guys. We go backstage and drink as much beer and whiskey as we can, play our shows, then hang back to watch the main act. The main act isn't bad, more a spectacle than anything else. The place is packed with a couple thousand screaming people throwing all kinds of shit around. The band members are puking on stage, spitting, jumping into the crowd, and doing their best Iggy Pop impersonations, whatever it takes. Music is not the important part of the show but nobody is here to listen intently anyway. They're here to throw stuff around and hopefully get laid. From the balcony where I'm standing, drink in hand, they look like a herd of wildebeest crossing the narrow part of a river. You can't say a meaningful word to a soul, not the time and place, never the time and place it seems for conversation. Conversation is dead and so is the exchanging of any useful ideas. No clear and coherent thought anywhere. All is dead here.

*A chlamys strewn about his otherwise naked body he strolled out of the wooden cabin overlooking the ravine. He seemed to radiate erudition as he approached. I noticed in his right hand a daruma doll, and in his left hand a hemimorphic object of some sort that shone brightly, reflecting the sun's rays in all directions. He approached calmly, resembling a Peloponnesian statesman, or did he resemble Pelagius the English monk, or Malachi the prophet?*

*Progress, as a rule, comes gradually. How many enlightened beings are presently walking among us? How many have found the way to full liberation and become pure-minded saintly people? Perhaps many, perhaps none. Surely many are walking a moral path and trying for complete mastery of the mind, a path towards wisdom and mind purification, and just as many must be walking a path that leads only to ignorance wrought by physical sloth and mental torpor, agitation and worry, doubt and uncertainty.*

*Ready to receive one and all with no prejudice. An orant with arms stretched to the heavens and feet pointing to hell. That is what I have always been after, it seems. An all-encompassing receiver with not a trace of penitence. Penis mind, cock mind, cunt mind, sentient and fecund, with no pendency. Ready to strike out or remain inward. Not cunning but prurient. Lusting after an imaginary psaltery-playing acrobat girl pushing supertonic notes down the hollow center of my spinal column. A Pangea-superstratum mind, supersonic and unfailing.*

# Brooklyn

The fat female cat we keep in the loft is hungry and loud but we will no longer feed it. Not until she performs her natural duty and catches a mouse or two. The damn mice are having a field day in our humble-looking kitchenette and we desperately require the fat female cat's services and hope she comes to her senses and contemplates the task at hand. Her predatory instincts will surely kick in after a few days or else she will starve to death. That is unless she realizes what kind of undisciplined and uncompassionate souls she is dealing with and abstains from killing another being. We might have a Buddhist cat on our hands after all. A cat well versed in metaphysics. A monk cat. We need a panther in here, a tigress unfamiliar with vegetarianism and nonviolence, an unfaithful and heathen feline, ferocious and wild, dangerous to the bone, with claws as sharp as a supersaurus, unemployable, unpredictable, intractable, and vicious. Her soul a fiery mass of hatred, her reflexes well honed, and a mind designed for one thing and one thing only: to kill, maim, and devour flesh. We need to see blood dripping from her fangs. We need her.

She resembles a tapir more than a cat, her excreta a foul-smelling mass with which we have to live. We need a precious catalyzer for this leonine, one that will act as a cellular illuminator. Maybe we'll take her on a trip to Japan, where, among other things, she can experience satori. She will kill again and with extreme regularity once she gets a full translocation of the mind, a transmogrification.

The kids are off to band rehearsal. Bands after all need to rehearse. Since I got back from med-camp there's been a few changes, we now have a woman living with us. Our home is a sanctuary, a place where all are welcome to practice or preach whatever their hearts desire. An artist's refuge of sorts where creation abounds and radiates in all directions, a kind of Hashshashin's fortress at Alamut, the embodiment of Hassan-i Sabbah's combined philosophies, minus the murder. We practice all sorts of sorcery here and mathematics, alchemy, medicine, botany, metempsychosis, devotional techniques. We drink zaffer and turpentine, milk and honey, water and wind, mead and mud.

We observe weightlessness and welding. We raise

our arms towards welkin, the sky, the vault of heaven, and howl fortissimo. We dilute our minds on a diurnal as well as a nocturnal schedule. The motion of the celestial bodies excites us constantly. Welfarism abounds here. We have our own imaginary San Andreas Fault.

Our new companion is an enigma of sorts, a Germanic/Persian hybrid well versed in psychology and polydipsia. Her thirst for life is unparalleled. She has climbed mountains and rock formations all over the world. Her sexual appetites are seemingly Noachian in nature. She needs a Tarzan lover, a task force, she needs to be uncorked, needs a war bonnet. Her odd and capricious desires must arrive at a zero-sum conclusion. She is a zenist approaching her zenith. The first time I looked into her eyes and saw a portion of her young soul it resembled the growth pattern of a mushroom, with fronts of arrest and waves of successive impulsions. She is, of course, a vegetarian. I will paint a vesica piscis of this vespertine vamp, improvise a capriccio, compose an allegro when my turn comes.

Out of range? Not even close. We're just rolling on down the line in a barrel like a bunch of demented monkeys and having a hell of a good time swallowing everything in sight. No watches, broken phones, free furniture, free booze and beer, family-style meals once a day, inviting the pretty neighbor girl over and forgetting about her boyfriend. Staying up until morning every night, arm around a different gal every other night (if possible) and telling them all about staying free from obligation. Women need to be reminded not to date musicians or at least to forget about any form of long-term commitment from them. Well, there are of course women musicians too, but that's a whole other story. There is a party and everyone is here, everything is happening, nothing is happening, no permanent solutions, dreams, and projections, I am free, you are free, we are free. But from what?

My alarm clock goes off at 5.45 a.m. I lie there in a daze and after realizing who, what, and where I am, get up and drag myself into the bathroom. The beard has to go. According to Koli's lawyer it is best not to resemble a terrorist when you walk into an office belonging to the Department of Homeland Security. I start to take my winter beard off then jump into the shower and pray to the hot-water gods to give me time to wash and condition my hair.

'My hair won't look like this tomorrow,' I had promised Koli's lawyer and her assistant the night before at our pre-hearing meeting.

'Good. You guys need to clean yourselves up. If you show up looking like this tomorrow I'm dropping the case,' the lawyer had said only half jokingly. We looked like musicians, as far as I was concerned, but you can't argue with a lawyer who has never lost a case of this kind. Sitting there in the lounge of the Roosevelt Hotel in midtown Manhattan, tired and hungover, listening to the endless stream of information, I was forced to quickly grasp the seriousness of the game at hand. I was to be the interpreter at the asylum hearing after all, with the important job of translating English into Farsi and back into English again. My Farsi is not as good as it should be, but Koli and I understand each other perfectly well.

'Now as we've already told you, we're trying to be as harsh as possible with you guys so you'll be ready for anything they can throw at you,' the assistant said before tearing into us: 'What about this?' and 'Oh, really? Your statement seems to indicate otherwise . . . and when was that date again? No, wait for the translation. Go ahead and translate please.'

Koli certainly had a strong case by all standards of the Universal Declaration of Human Rights but, hey, you never know what can go wrong at these things, according to the attorneys. My head was threatening to explode with all the information and the constant switches between languages. My circulatory system was already in bad shape from a bout of heavy drinking the night before at a renowned Iranian-American artist's home. The kids (which kids?) were there too and it had been an okay night. I had played a few songs at the host's request and so had a few others. The wine and liquor were flowing, it was a good time, but now they were having grievous effects on me after only one or two hours of sleep and a full day at the office to pay the bills.

The left atrium of my heart wasn't getting the proper amount of blood, and apparently my pulmonary vein needed something it wasn't getting. That was my self-diagnosis, anyway, and I couldn't wait to move on to the self-medication phase. After about three hours the attorneys were finished with us and sent us home with lots of homework and last-minute fact-finding missions, omissions to the official statement, and lots of material for memorization. Koli seemed to prematurely age a few years. We don't fall asleep at normal hours, Koli normally goes to bed around 8 a.m., so there was no point in trying to sleep. We decided to gobble up as much speed as we could and push it all the way through to the next day. Hell, the more meek and distressed Koli looked, the better, right? He was after all supposed to be afraid for his life. If he gets sent back he'll be imprisoned. As soon as the plane lands in Tehran he'll be seized and dragged through the streets to be publicly flogged and later hanged in the center of town. Or that was the way I understood it anyway and my job as the translator called for me to put myself in Koli's place and feel every ounce of fear he felt.

This was no joking matter. This was the moment of

truth. One gets more than a single chance for asylum but after a first rejection the odds for success naturally diminish a bit, so it was absolutely imperative that we charmed the pants off of the judge or agent or whatever they call themselves to get this young man asylum in these here United States.

So we stayed up all night and memorized his statement, which was almost forty pages long, with many names, dates, and places to remember. By 5 a.m. I was beginning to feel a little sideways so I smoked some hash and told Koli to make sure I was awake in time to take a shower.

'You want to eat some breakfast?' Koli asked me after I got out of the shower.

'Shit, no, just give me another pill. I can't eat anything yet,' I said.

The asylum office is out in the boondocks, all the way out on the edge of Queens. It's a hell of a weird place to make all the immigrants go to beg for their lives. I really wonder what kind of a sadistic bastard picked the location. It's one of those office buildings that were built all over America in the eighties, you can see them all over Dallas for example or Atlanta, Charlotte, anywhere really, and it reflects that decade's monumental obsession with ugliness, greed, and efficiency – in America anyway. In the lobby, which sports a semi-atrium, there are horrendous copies of Greek statues, fake plants, a non-working fountain, and a dirty diner that serves cheap food. All appointments are set very early in the morning and if you're late then you're fucked. That's one of the reasons they put the office way the hell out there I think. There is no subway stop close by. You have to take the subway to the end of the line then transfer to a bus for a forty-five-minute ride out to the edge of the city for a 7 a.m. appointment. But hey, if you want to stay in the US then you better do what it takes, right? We were taking the kids' van and didn't have to concern ourselves with public transportation but it was still hard to find the place even with the GPS on Koli's phone. We got there with a minute or so to spare and waited in the long line with all the other immigrants. Most of the people looked to be Chinese, many others were from Arab nations, and of course there were many Africans too.

'Take everything out of your pockets and place it in the bin, take off your belts, have your ID in hand,' a very large and serious black female security guard was yelling at everybody.

'Hey, it's the Beatles,' she said with a big flirtatious smile as she passed us. Koli and I smiled and nodded back at her.

Once past the security we sat down in the waiting area and waited for Koli's lawyers to arrive.

'You better give me another one of those pills,' I told Koli, and he did before saying, 'Look at all the

Chinese, they're dressed like they don't give a shit.'

'They don't,' I said before swallowing the pill. 'Look at them, it's one lawyer per ten or fifteen of them. They come over here as indentured servants basically and their boss gets them a cheap lawyer while they work off their insurmountable debt. Hell, they can get rejected and keep working illegally, it doesn't matter. Look how relaxed and uninterested they all are. That's the look you get when you're fucked on all fronts.'

'Yeah, well, I'm scared shitless,' Koli said.

'Good, good. Stay that way,' I said.

Just then the lawyers arrived. Koli was paying a steep price for his legal counsel, they were not here to disappoint, and looked like they meant serious business. Also they were showing lots of leg and cleavage.

'I hope we have a male judge, Koli, look at these two.'

'Yeah, they look about ready, don't they?' he said.

The lawyer and her assistant sat down next to us and were impressed by the way we looked as well.

'You guys cleaned up very nicely,' the lawyer said, and her assistant confirmed this by nodding. Everybody in the place was now staring at us. Who are these people? they seemed to be saying. We looked like a serious case. The look on the judge/agent of the Department of Homeland Security's face when he came out to greet us was one of bewilderment and excitement. From this point forward I can't say much about what happened unless I want to violate my confidentiality agreement with high-powered lawyers and the United States government, but I can say that it was one theatrical hoot. The trip we laid on the poor agent, all true of course, was one for the ages. He didn't know what to make of all the grim details reminiscent of Nazi interrogation techniques, along with ghastly tales of imprisonment, torture, and a campaign by the Iranian government to wreak havoc on a young man's life and all others like him. Needless to say, we felt pretty confident walking out of that office after about six hours of back and forth questioning, with very few breaks in between.

'Let's celebrate,' the lawyer said. 'Drinks on me.' Which of course meant that the drinks were on Koli's tab, but what the hell, he has a rich father.

'You're pretty good at this interpreting thing,' the assistant said to me on the way to the van.

'Yeah, I'm seeing a bright future ahead. I can rent a kiosk at JFK and snatch them up right after they step off the plane. Charge five hundred bucks a head and make a thriving business for myself. I'll of course need plenty of legal counsel before then so I guess we'll be in touch.'

# Shiraz

I salute the dead of the war that engulfed the better part of my childhood, the children especially, for they were the lucky ones. I on the other hand have never known luck and was spared. In the years that followed and through some fiendish thought process I was made to feel lucky to exist, but to my thinking the lucky ones were taken away with the bombs and the bullets, the gas and the missiles. They went right back to the eternal comforts of the spirit world.

Those bombs took my boyhood too. I will forever be frightened of their thunderously devilish sounds and monstrously hideous mushroom-cloud hellfires, which start blood red at the bottom, and centrifugally climb towards the heavens, only to turn black as night. A child can never understand war. Why then should a grown-up? Not the economic damage mind you, or the socio-political. Not the human loss or displacement factor but the incalculable spiritual damage, the marching backwards, the inverse growth, the atrophy. A child can mourn infinitely more than an adult can.

A silent mourning, a feeble, all-encompassing, all-possessing, eternal mourning. A child understands only too soon what kind of a world he or she has entered, and no matter how many stupid faces the adults make the child finds it difficult to laugh. They only do so to indulge the dumb adults.

Back then, during the war, I used to wake up screaming every night. I mean hair-raising, top-of-the-lungs, parents-come-running-in, sweat-pouring-down-body screams. I must have been nine or ten and being the oldest took myself rather seriously for a kid. Forcing my mother or father to run in and comfort me every night wasn't my idea of fun. We lived, for most of the war, in the city of Shiraz. My father was in the Air Force so we lived on base, on the fifth floor of an officers' building. The building was supposedly bomb-resistant from the third floor down and so when the nightly warning sirens sounded at three or four in the morning, my mother would wake us kids up and take us down to the first floor.

Walking down the stairs, which were on the front of the building and exposed, you could see the anti-aircraft guns shooting their bright red loads into the night sky from many different locations all over the city, the shells rat-tat-tatting in a red glowing row upwards before exploding, one after another, a few thousand feet above us. These things never hit any planes as far as I could see since the enemy planes flew just above their range and dropped a few bombs then escaped as fast as possible to avoid an encounter with one of our fighter jets. Those particular bombs would damage a few homes or set fire to a whole city block because of gas explosions. It wasn't like London in World War II or Vietnam, where a few squadrons of planes came every night, but one or two jets did come every night, or every other night, or whenever, that was the whole point: they were going to come, if not tonight then tomorrow night. That is what you call psychological warfare, it is primarily focused on the civilian population, and of course it works best on children. When we got down to the first floor we went inside someone else's home, the neighbor's, an officer and his wife, with kids, who not only had to worry about their own lot, but all of a sudden twenty or thirty others filling their hallways.

The lights went out in the whole city as soon as the sirens sounded. The power company flipped the switch and BAM! all was dark. No one was allowed to strike a match, turn on a flashlight, flash a gold-toothed grin, nothing, because even a little light was supposed to be visible when the entire city was dark, and you didn't want to give the enemy pilots a visual target. We'd all pile in a hallway with no outside walls and sit it out. The sounds of exploding bombs were inevitable. Sound is just as intense miles away from the epicenter. Those thunderous sounds meant only one thing, death and destruction. The whole charade was over in ten or fifteen minutes.

In the morning we'd go off to school like normal kids and practice bomb drills at random intervals three or four times a day. The teachers made sure we took these drills seriously and came down hard on any horseplay. Most of us didn't care much. They'd never be able to hit the base, we all figured, until one day they did hit the base and the high school directly behind our elementary school. My friend Reza and I were among the first to walk in the classroom after recess that day when the sirens went off. Normally you'd get two or three minutes after the sirens to duck for cover, but this time the sound of exploding bombs came hard and fast, shattering the glass in our classroom as we all fell to the floor. Reza was close to the window and I can still remember his frightened nine-year-old face as glass shattered all around him and covered his body and scratched his cheeks. Later on we heard how many high-school kids had died but I don't remember being sad about the whole affair. I do, however, remember feeling lucky.

I can recount many incidents. I've seen planes drop bombs half a mile away from me. I've seen gigantic, mind-bending, black smoke clouds after they hit the oil refinery twenty miles away. There was a time when ballistic missiles were in vogue and you could see them flying overhead on a daily basis. The TV was full of images from the battle front too. I remember lots and lots of things. It was day in and day out for eight years, and we were right in the thick of it. Everybody was wrapped up in it and you heard countless stories. There was always some friend's father whose plane had crashed or been shot down. I even saw one crash and blow up right in front of my eyes. The next day we'd make sure the kid who'd just lost a father got picked first for the soccer match or a piece of candy and condolences.

I remember thinking how lucky I was that my father kept surviving his flight missions but the thing I understood about luck back then was that it could run out at any moment. That understanding must have led to a bunch of anxieties, hence the screaming every night, I suppose. It wasn't just the war either. The entire foundation of the country was shaken in those days.

I eventually stopped screaming every night. Leaving Iran must have helped. Germany was much different. Being an immigrant, although it presented its own set of challenges, was much better than living in a volatile place like Iran. I used to be such a clean-cut kid back then, a model student, but in Germany everything changed. I guess I knew my luck could run out at any moment so I started running around with the wild kids. As far as I was concerned there was no security anywhere. Everything can come to a fiery and meaningless end at any moment, for no reason at all, or none that can really be explained satisfactorily. Germany would eventually come to an end too and it was off to America. America! America! It was all very unbelievable, and for a while very difficult, and I always wondered, as I still do, when it would all come to an end.

It ain't that easy. You can't just turn it off. I have a heart. It's covered in cobwebs and suffers from bad plumbing (genetics, cocaine, cigarettes, alcohol, stress, no exercise, etc.) but hell it's a damn good heart. I got it a thousand years ago and it's still the same after all this time.

# Toronto

The kids are finishing an interview with a Canadian film crew who are doing a documentary on underground Iranian rock music. The interviewer keeps asking them about politics and the underground ideal of staying pure. The kids don't want to stay pure in that way, keep saying that they have no desire to, that they were only underground because they weren't able to legally play rock music in Iran. The Canadians just don't understand.

'But you do have a political cause?' they keep asking. I finally have to step in and straighten the Canucks out.

'They don't care about the political situation, they are apolitical, they're just musicians,' I say. 'Oh, but come on, surely they have an opinion on the illegal Iranian elections etc.,' they keep saying. 'No, they don't, they're just musicians.' They finally leave without getting the point. but what the hell, they get grants from their government to make their documentaries.

'I think something is wrong with my dick,' Siamak is telling us at the table. We're smoking a joint, didn't have any money to buy the weed ourselves so I went to our French neighbors for a little handout.

'What's wrong with your dick?' I ask.

'It's kind of swollen,' he says sheepishly.

'Any red bumps on it?' I inquire further.

'No. It's just red and swollen, itches a little.' He'd been with a new girl all weekend, a go-go dancer. She's a loud one.

'Siamak, you've gotta wash your cock,' I say to him.

'Ha?'

'What, you think you can just go at it all day and night without a break? After a good fuck excuse yourself and throw a little water on the little fella then wipe it dry. Freshen it up a bit,' I advise.

'Oh, yeah?' he says.

'Yeah! Hell, they used to powder their cocks back in the day,' I say, and the kids laugh.

'Listen to your elders, you dirty bastard,' Koli tells Siamak. 'Ali, he's a lost cause. It's a wonder a girl can even stand next to him long enough for anything else to happen the way he smells. You stink, Siamak! Wash his cock? Wash, period! Wash yourself, you dirty son of a bitch!'

They love to give Siamak hell, don't want him to get a big head being the lead singer and all. He takes it in good stride and always tries to give a little back without much success.

'She's a dirty little whore anyway,' Manuchehr says.

'Where did you find such a whorish bitch this time?'

'I like whores, don't you remember? And they like me.'

'Of course, whores love a man with no morals and a deep pocket. Let me know when it's my turn with her, will you? Don't wear her out now. Shit, you fuck like a goddamn camel. I thought you were killing her at one point.'

Sometimes when your rhythm gets disrupted all hell breaks loose. In the middle of me running around New York and doing my best playboy act I had to go to Toronto for thirteen days as part of a new musical project that would put some money in my pocket. One of Dari's bandmates, Sheerdaad, had convinced me to sing with him for money. He is a brute of a man with brutal aspirations for world domination and a hard-on for some cheap tramp up there in Canada. The bastard had promised me adequate lodging with one of his dear friends, a woman, who would give me my own room and cook lavish meals at all hours of the day and night. I should have never trusted the greedhead, but I guess I was a little greedy myself, mainly for money of course. When you get hungry, you get weird and disgruntled, and nobody can judge you for your sins unless they are hungry themselves.

Sheerdaad gave me directions to his friend's place and went to diddle his girlfriend. I took a streetcar and after a while was knocking on the door of a total stranger, who not only couldn't offer me anything more than a couch in the middle of her studio apartment but was also on a diet and not cooking anything, for anybody, at any hour. I felt pretty nasty about the whole affair from the get-go but there was no choice other than to stay and play nice. Somewhere along the line, after having to sleep in the stranger's home, with barely any money, and no suitable clothing to combat the freezing temperatures of a Toronto autumn, my mojo slowly drained away. I lost the killer instinct for love or business.

Sheerdaad was no help to me at all and there was some kind of silent agreement among the women, who came and went in the groups I was introduced to, that I was off limits. Most of the people we were hanging around with were Iranians. They all knew each other, and hung out on a regular basis. In a situation like that a woman would be branded a whore for life for even pretending to do something with an outsider. These things run deep in the Iranian culture and even the most modern Iranians suffer from these defects. For some reason the Iranian woman forgets she has a vagina sometimes, or maybe she suddenly remembers what brutes us Iranian men can be.

There really was nothing for me to do up there. I had been to Toronto several times before to play in festivals and wasn't exactly fond of the place to begin with. It's not one of those cities that offer much in the form of architectural eye candy. I had played it cool up until the night of the show, with women anyways, but was definitely ready for some action afterward. There was one girl who after the gig was seemingly ready to sacrifice her tribal ties but logistical problems got in the way. I had to pack up the gear and go with Sheerdaad and his girl to her friend's house to drop everything off, then to the bar she wanted to go to on the other side of town. My uneasy coked-up state coupled with starvation and too much whiskey was beginning to turn me into a hard man to deal with, and of course people were bumping into me for no reason at all.

'Excuse me! Oh no, excuse me, fella! Hey, you just stepped on me . . . Well, if you'd get the hell out of my way . . .'

I was in no mood for a Canadian brawl so I mumbled a quick goodbye to Sheerdaad and his girl before taking three or four taxis around town to the houses of random people who'd invited me over after the show, and tried to connect with one of them who said he had lots of cocaine and wanted to party. I just had to wait for him there for an hour. Of course he arrived after all the girls, pardon me, the only available girl had left with her friend and her friend's pompous boyfriend. The guy whose studio apartment I finally ended up at was a nice enough fellow but a fiend for useless discussions about the things people who are comfortable financially and socially like to discuss for hour upon endless hour.

'Listen,' I finally said to him. 'Fuck Ahmadinejad, fuck the Iranian government, fuck the United Nations, and fuck you! Okay? You really have no idea what you're talking about. Call me long distance in a few days in New York. I'll give you a real earful that'll *really* give you a hard-on for this stuff. You're a nice rich boy, so stick to your high-powered job in the Canadian Ministry of Whatever the Fuck It's Called and shut the fuck up, will you?'

He didn't like that very much but it didn't make much difference. By then the late-fall sun was just about to rise up from behind Lake Ontario. The water was clearly visible through the wall-to-wall windows of my new friend's twenty-third-floor apartment. What the hell, eh? I had drunk at least four or five tall glasses of absinthe on the rocks with a splash of water at his place and badly needed the cocaine to keep awake, for what God only knew. Well, my friend who brought the coke soon got the idea to go to a whorehouse. Oh well, I had all that cash from the show burning a hole in my pocket, so what the hell, right?

Then it was, 'How about this place . . . what about her . . . and I have a friend,' and all that until it became painfully obvious that six o'clock on a Saturday morning in Toronto was not prime time for finding prostitutes for some odd reason. None of the massage parlors or bathhouses were even open.

'Jesus Christ! What kind of a lame country is this? Shit, in New York, New Orleans, or even Nashville you can find a brothel at all hours of the day and night! And you guys keep comparing this city to New York?' I was yelling.

We went to the Internet for help. After much deliberation we settled on an Asian girl who promised us several times over the phone that she was the girl in the photo.

'Okay, I'm gonna ask you one last time just so we have no misunderstandings. Are you sure you are the girl in the photo? Because I will not let you in, okay . . . Yes, two guys for sure and maybe a third guy,' my friend said firmly.

'She swears she's the one.'

'There is no way in hell she's that girl, I'll bet you the price of a fuck she's not the one,' the politics freak added confidently.

'Well, she's on her way over. By the way, I'm gonna be short of a little cash. I have my card of course . . .'

'It's okay, I'll cover you,' I said stupidly. The guy drove a Porsche and owned real estate all over Toronto and there I was picking up his hooker tab.

A little while later we were taking the elevator down to get her, she was standing behind the door, looking okay enough at a glance, the body was nice. A closer look, the face was not the best, but not the worst either. She was not the girl from the photo.

'Hello,' my friend said.

'Ah, hello,' she answered. Her English was barely decipherable.

We took her up in the elevator and into the room. She was playful the whole time, but as soon as we got inside and she took off her coat and hat, the subject of money came up immediately. She had to have the money then, which was of course understandable, but she wasn't satisfied with only two guys.

'You say tree, not two. I come for tree.'

'No, what I said was maybe three,' my friend said firmly.

The matter got settled quickly and it was on again.

'Okay, let's go. Who? You?' she said, pointing to me, but I shook my head.

'Come on, have some coke first,' my friend said.

'Ooh, coke? No.'

'Yes, come on,' he insisted.

She did some and had a shot of vodka. I let my friend go first. I wasn't up for it yet. She was too business-minded. A good prostitute knows how to make you feel right about the experience, knows what you want, makes you a lifelong customer. Well, not this one, she was all about math and mechanics. So they went to the room and stayed there for about thirty minutes. She was screaming for the most part as he pounded away at her. By the time they were done she was royally fucked out and appeared to be practically another person. My turn. We went in. She wanted to get right down to it.

'Why don't you take five minutes and relax?' I said gently.

'No,' she said firmly, took down my pants and started to blow me in the most mechanical way possible. I stopped her quickly and asked her again to just relax for a minute and let me do the same. She wouldn't hear of it.

'Listen, just forget the whole thing. It ain't gonna happen. You can go,' I told her after a few minutes of failure, and she left.

I woke up a few hours later on the pull-out couch bed with the sun in my eye, and cast a frightened, beaten glance over the lake. Parts closer to shore were frozen already. It looked lonely and cold, like death. Most of my money was gone and thoughts of the future sent nervous shivers up my spine, but at least everything was honest.

I really am wretched and incapable of doing anything right. I can't help myself.

I had to get the hell out of Toronto and back home to New York after that. The whole goddamned trip was a mistake. I felt like a monkey up on stage. You see, the goal had been to make money from our own people, the Iranian diaspora, which we had done. But Iranians for the most part are to be avoided at all cost. You'd be hard pressed to find very many rock 'n' rollers among them. I had made damn sure to be the craziest one in the room wherever I went and had, for the most part, succeeded in doing so. Something in the basic fabric of Iranians makes us deeply mistrustful of each other's motives. I had always tried to avoid this pitfall but it eventually caught up with me too, I guess.

Now it was time to head back and pick up the pieces back home. There would hopefully be some work waiting for me when I got back. I said goodbye to Sheerdaad and the rest of the folks while trying to finish off the coke I had left over from the night before. The bus took off at 11 p.m. Eastern Standard Time and I was completely wired. There was still a lot left in the little baggie and I had planned to finish it off on the bus via several trips to the bus bathroom. After the second or third trip I noticed my dilated pupils in the mirror and recoiled in horror. The border was only about an hour away and the customs agents awaited me with candor and delight. I was already in trouble with the bastards. My entry into Canada had been a disorderly one.

'Do you have a return ticket?' the female border agent had asked me.

'No.'

'How much cash do you have on you, sir?'

'Oh, not much. Thirty bucks or so.'

'Any credit cards?'

'No.'

'Follow me please.'

She took me through some doors to the other side.

'Wait here for the next available agent,' she said.

What? Where? When, Lord? I waited in line until it was time to approach the counter.

'What is your reason for visiting Canada?' asked a pale-faced agent.

'Oh, just visiting friends.'

'Are you traveling with anyone and when do you plan on going back?'

'No, alone and I'm going back in a couple of weeks or so.'

'How do you plan on supporting yourself and how will you buy the return ticket?'

'I have a friend who'll loan me some money.'

The whole charade fell apart rather quickly after that. You see, Sheerdaad and I had decided, at his request, not to mention the fact that we were traveling together and going up there to play a show so we wouldn't need a work visa and could avoid paying taxes. The agent started to ask me about where I was staying, and when he called the man who I had never met but was supposedly staying with, he only got Sheerdaad's name as a reference.

'Well, he said nothing about you staying there, but who is Sheerdaad?'

'Oh, right . . . He's my friend . . . on the same bus. I realize I haven't mentioned him but isn't traveling together like when you are with a family member or your wife or something?' I said, feigning ignorance.

'No, sir, traveling together means simply that. Traveling with someone.'

'Oh, well. Sorry. Look, I don't know too many people up there. I just needed to get away from New York for a while and meet some new people. Other artists, you understand . . .'

'This is not good. Your story doesn't check out.'

'Look, there is no story. I don't want to stay in Canada. I am an American. I live in New York City and I want to die there if at all possible,' I said, feeling a bit edgy now.

'I'm sorry sir . . . this—'

'Can't I prove to you that I'm leaving? I mean, I don't want to stay in Canada!' I interrupted him rudely.

After a whole lot more hullabaloo he decided to grant me entry provided that I make a U-turn at the border upon leaving and check in with Canadian customs. This was the only way they could be sure that I'd left their beloved Canada. He would only let me stay for two weeks. Then he stamped my beautiful blue

American passport and sent me on my merry way.

Now on the return leg of my trip I was staring at my dilated pupils in the filthy bus bathroom mirror with thoughts drifting towards some nasty possibilities. Those customs rooms are always brightly lit, I thought, so the bastards can have a really good look at you, and there was still a hell of a lot of coke left to snort. I wasn't entirely comfortable with myself.

I went back to my seat and tried to relax for a second.

There was nowhere to hide the coke, or was there? They certainly walk through the bus with a drug dog, but are they only looking for big amounts of drugs, and what happens if they find a little coke anyway? Do they question the entire bus, old ladies and all? What if they do and get to me and see my bugged-out eyes? Is there a drug test involved? 'It's my cold medicine, officer, they put speed in the capsules. Yes, I have a cold. Can't you see me sniveling?' That would be my only excuse.

Forget it. First things first. Watching all that good cocaine being flushed down by the blue liquid in the bus toilet was a heartbreaker of epic proportions. A thoroughly lonesome feeling washed over my body, mind, and soul. On my first trip to Canada a few years back I had accidentally snuck some weed in and no one had noticed at customs – why couldn't I sneak some cocaine through as well? The bus pulled up to the border station, we all got out and waited in line for questioning. The guy in front of me got drilled rather viciously and so did a few others with foreign passports. Look calm, cool, and collected, like a good Christian, a messenger of the Lord back from the true north after having spread the message, like a prodigal son coming back home to continue his evangelical duties. Tough sale? Hell, Jesus hung out with scoundrels and prostitutes, the lowest of the low! What's wrong with a junkie preacher?

'Why were you in Canada?' asked the fat slob of a man from behind his pestiferous counter. He had a white mustache and murderous eyes like most border agents.

'Oh, just visiting friends,' I said in my best American accent.

'Where are you going?'

'New York City.'

'Why?'

'I live there.'

'Do you have more than a thousand dollars cash on you?'

'I wish,' I chuckled.

'Oh, yeah?' he asked as if surprised, then started to look more closely at my passport. 'What is your ethnicity?'

Oh, dear Lord, I thought. Here we go.

'Turkish?' he asked.

'My parents are Iranian but as you can see . . .'

'Oh, I just like to guess these things for my own benefit. Doesn't matter anyways, you're an American citizen,' he said without looking up. Sure thing, officer, you crummy shit. Then he threw my passport down in front of me.

'Do I get a welcome home, officer?' I asked him with an all-American smile.

'Sure,' he said, without saying welcome home.

After all that I didn't give a flying fuck about going back to the Canadian side to check back in with them, or out with them, or whatever the hell they wanted me to do. Damn the consequences. Add one more potential calamity to the long list. I didn't care to ever step foot into Canada again unless the Native Americans of the Six Nations of the Grand River First Nation were giving amnesty to people like me. It was damn good to be back in the US of A, my home, the land I love no matter how many things are wrong with it. Whatever it is, it's better than a hell of a lot of other places and it's not like I was going back to Butte, Montana, or El Paso, or even Los Angeles for that matter. I was going back home to New York for better or worse.

# Brooklyn

The kids and I often play music together at the loft and their rehearsal space. The music is good, but for some reason they don't want to move forward with anything tangible. I can't blame them, maybe it's the age difference or maybe they know me well enough by now and know I won't play the game right.

Lying there on my bed in the middle of the loft and thinking about the human condition, which is to say my own condition, really. No one is here for once and the place is quiet. Always on the run, eh? Always planning another trip, bags perpetually packed and ready. Maybe I can jump on a freight train and go to Wyoming, take that ship to Argentina, join the merchant marines, go work on an organic farm somewhere – anything but this.

*My mind bends inward towards the fifth dimension. Many geometric possibilities become visible and apparent. Ancient forces take over inside of me. I am a vessel. A ship reserved for energy transport across space and time. I am overflowing with karmic lava spraying out of every pore. My outer crust remains intact while my inner core burns to ash. Get up, put your pants on and leave, I command you. The world is your rightful home and you are free to roam, free to walk upon it. I see myself as I once was, can feel it, am it. There is work to be done. One must not give up. My mind is splintering in a thousand different directions at once, concentration fragmentation, mind exploding, shrapnel everywhere, mushroom clouds, 5th grade lunch room, Germany, Iran, bombs, Texas summers, extreme heat, air conditioning, alternating current, Nikola Tesla, direct current, synthetic souls, rubber masks, money, bills, coins, mother, death, life, birth, joy, sorrow, white-sand beaches, vacations, tarantulas, iguanas, snakes, serpent wings of the death wizard, angelic sirens of the doomed clock-tower people, nomadic humdrum, expedient practitioners of the northern hemisphere's atmospheric and oceanic theorems, voodoo people, headhunters of the Amazon, French Papua New Guinea, Fiji, Addis Ababa, the great Zagros mountains, Mount Zion, Jesus, Judas, Mary Magdalene, the apostles, Zarathustra, lightning and thunder in the desert, the great flood.*

*Noah, oh Noah, I came to know your name as Nooh. I was told your story as a boy. I spoke a different language then, completely unaware of my destiny, my final end, my calling, my duty. I cared not what it was just yet but did have visions of grandiose proportions. I dreamt and day-dreamt regularly that I was a prophet child, the next chosen one, the preordained being of light and darkness, the shower, the instrument, the bearer of great knowledge, a martyr, ready to die on whatever death machine necessary.*

The door opens, my thoughts freeze, I'm hurled back into my body, pull the covers over my head quickly, and try to act like I'm asleep. In walk Siamak and Allison talking about something or other. I haven't seen her since I left for Canada. Siamak goes to his room while Allison goes to the bathroom. I can hear her pissing. It turns me on for some strange reason. I can't pretend to be asleep. I want to lay her down on the dining table and lick her from head to toe. She walks out of the bathroom.

'Hi, Allison,' I say.

'Hey, you! Did we wake you up?' she says.

'It's okay, how are you?'

'I'm good, we were out at a bar, thought we'd come up here for a few beers.'

'It's great to see you,' I say with a smile.

Siamak comes back. I pretend to want to leave them alone but they're okay with me hanging out. Allison takes out a little baggie of cocaine and in the process of scooping some out with a key spills the whole thing in her purse. She's very upset about it so we try to calm her down and salvage as much as possible. In a flash we're sticking straws in her purse and sniffing out as much as we can, laughing at ourselves the whole time. She gets a phone call. Something terrible has happened.

'My grandmother just passed away, down in Florida,' she says.

'God, I'm so sorry, are you . . . ?' I say.

She starts to cry, then stops herself. 'I'm sorry to ruin the . . .'

'Are you kidding? You're amongst friends, cry all you want, we're here for you,' I say, and Siamak concurs. A little while later, after she's talked a bit about her grandmother and calmed down, she's speaking of leaving. Siamak goes to his room to get something. It's now or never.

'Well, you look very beautiful. It's great to see you even on such a tragic night,' I say to her.

'Thanks,' she says and asks if she can have my number. I give it to her as Siamak is walking out of his room. She leaves.

'Siamak, she asked for my number, I didn't ask for hers.'

'Don't worry about it.'

'Are you sure? Because . . .'

'Yeah, really, I think we're just friends anyway.'

'Are you *sure*?'

'Yeah, yeah.'

Well, he said he was sure and I was going to take his word for it.

I was going to run to her the first chance I got, had to make her mine, wanted to be hers. The next few times we met it was always hard to pin her down. We both had lots of loose ends to tie up if we were to continue down the line together. Our first date involved five or six bars in a few hours, no money, snow, her falling down, asking some dude in her little group who was clearly after her if he could 'buy a drink for my friend and me.' The guy said he'd only buy a drink for her. I was embarrassed and told her never to do that again.

'I don't have any money but that doesn't mean I want a handout from that cocksucker.'

At the last bar we go to she asks the bartender for a free drink.

'Well, if you're gonna ask,' the female bartender says, 'I'm gonna give it to you.' Ha! What a line, eh? That was easy. For the first time in my life I'm jealous of other men, don't want them anywhere near her. Men and women can't be friends, I keep saying to her, this is serious, I keep repeating. We had to build a fortress in the middle of it all, had to protect our love and let it flourish, had to cut off the fat, sever ties with good-timing friends, leeches, withdraw from the flesh piste, filtrate the waters, aim the sails into the wind and towards dry land. I was tired of lurking in the dark, needed to stop the dynamo. Had to let go and surrender. Needed to tap into the primitive self. To swim in the Tigris and bathe in the Euphrates, to walk between the great rivers and bask in the glorious sunlight which long ago warmed the bodies of the ancients.

I was rapidly becoming a man: a lover, a builder, a hunter, a thief, a scoundrel, a leader of revolts, an adventurer, a court jester, a king, a commoner, a slave, a shepherd, a singer of hymns.

I could picture the little ones running around, could picture her as an old woman, didn't care about anything else. What the hell else is there anyway? We can do anything we want, Allison, I keep saying to her. Go anywhere we want. Mornings, bright mornings, Allison. Light, Allison, bright light. I keep talking, keep going to her, waiting for her to come to me. Backwards, forwards, left, and right, like a crab, Allison. Rockiest mountain passes, driest deserts, sandstorms, torrential rains, monsoons, magnetic force disruptions, solar rays, Allison. Apocalyptic ends, atom heart core, Allison.

On a snowy winter's day with the city covered in white we lie down next to each other and all seems to be working right. She kisses me and within a moment we are melting into one another. Our tongues are intertwined, slow dancing, gently massaging, caressing, artfully tracing invisible patterns, manipulating, morphing, palpating. Eyes closed, lucid, a pleasure penumbra fluctuating between us. Holding each other tightly, I grab the back of her head, she rubs her crotch against my leg, I push myself against her, then the two magnets meet head on and rub against one another. I reach down into her jeans and rub her bare ass. It's smooth as silk. Breathing heavy now, accelerated heartbeat, flashes of light, strobes in the medulla, plutonium in the veins, chain reactions, neutrons colliding. My hand slips a little farther down her pants and curves around her ass. She swings her legs open in the other direction to make herself more accessible. The tips of my fingers feel the top of her pubic region. She's hot, ready for action, ready for the plunge, the finality of existence. My body's entire supply of the somatotropic hormone is being redirected to my cock. My finger is now bathing in her juices. She unbuttons my jeans, takes down the zipper, and reaches in for me. I could explode like a volcano. She lifts up her shirt and exposes her breasts, nipples erect, grabs the back of my head and pushes it towards her. I lick and suck. Her pants must come off, she must be naked, we must be naked. Her pants come off, my jeans come off, shirts off, she pulls me on top of her. We're looking deep into each other's eyes again. Within a moment I find myself inside her.

*Complete symmetry, magnetism, changing electric field, interplanetary travel, all the world sucked into a vacuum, billions of light years this side of the present and that side of it, God and man, migrating herds, cosmic rays, monoliths, elastic distortions of reality, cave paintings, desert survival, mass exodus across the great land bridge, alternating charge, all of history swirling around, multi-dimensional thoughts barely decipherable but completely understood and forgotten in a flash. God and man. Universe and man. Mother Earth and man. Man and woman. Woman and God. Woman. God. Billions of years. Ancient souls. No past, no future, only the present. Only now. Right now. Here. Nothingness, infinity, tears. Understanding not with the brain. No brain. No gut. Nothingness. Nil. No language. Zero. Negative, positive. Reversals. Now. Here. Tick . . . tock. Time. What time? What is time? Now. Here. Right here . . . and there as well, everywhere . . .*

'It's raining cunt out there,' says Koli in Farsi so that only us Iranians in the van will understand. 'It's Cunt Boulevard, Cunt Square!' he says as we drive down Berry Street in Brooklyn. We're driving to the beach, the whole family plus a couple of Allison's friends, American girls from North Africa. We've been at it for a couple of solid weeks. Lots of parties at the house, lots of late nights. Lots of speed, coke, and hash, plus the Tramadol, and music. This yuppie pot dealer who is a recent transplant from Massachusetts has been selling us the hash.

The kids and I are old druggies, so is Allison for that matter, and old druggies know to stagger doses. We know to watch the upper/downer combinations. We're not going out like some actor in distress or an old singer who can't sleep. Also, drugs should always remain secondary to the task at hand. Drugs can enhance an experience but will never fill your water well if it's drying up. They are not an oasis in the middle of the desert. It's wonderful to be at the beach. Allison and I have made vegetarian sandwiches for all to enjoy. We run into the waves, the waves crash against us, we embrace, run, splash, swim, we laugh and scream. Lying there on the sand my thoughts drift away while the waves sing and the sun warms our half-naked bodies.

Coming back from the beach and smoking hash in the van now. Allison is touching me with everyone around but no one can see anything. We get back home and do it in the shower. Later we go out for a few drinks and she gets her phone stolen. A mobster-looking guy at the bar says he'll drive me around in his Mercedes to look for the guys he thinks pulled the job. He wants to restore order in his neighborhood.

'There he is!' he says, after driving around the Lower East Side for a while. 'That's the guy. You better go talk to him.' He pulls over and waits for me to get out.

'Hey, man, I'm not a thief, man, I sell pills, that's what I was doing in that bar.' The tall but scrawny kid says this to me after I corner him, not in a cop-like manner, but rather cordially.

'Pills, eh? Well, whatcha got?' I say.

'Vicodin,' says the kid.

'Yeah? How much you selling 'em for?'

'Five bucks a piece.'

'Hmm, shit, I'll take four,' I say.

'You know what that looked like from here, don't you?' the mobster says to me with a smirk after I get back in the car. 'Like you two were in cahoots.'

He is right of course and it must have looked pretty suspicious from his vantage point, but hell, if the price is right you've got to make your move.

'Well, what do you propose we do? You're so dissatisfied with the state of things . . . coming from the country you come from, I mean you couldn't even say these things where you come from. What is your solution?' The manager's girlfriend is asking me this after she interrupted a conversation I was having with our Hungarian doctor.

'First of all I don't have a solution. Who am I? All I'm saying is we should think about what is happening to us as human beings and discuss it like grown-ups. And that's a right which this country gives its citizens, so yeah, I know where I come from and therefore I'm exercising my rights.'

'Well, you're complaining but don't have a solution,' she says.

'All I'm saying is we should think and act collectively, that's all. We shouldn't wait for politicians or governments.'

You have to become invisible. Got to hide away from people or they'll eat out your guts and make furniture with your bones. You'll end up as a chair in a garage sale.

'How much for that bone chair?' some passerby asks half-heartedly.

'Eh, that one? It's been in our family for a few years now . . . How about two dollars?' the guy standing in front of his open garage answers distractedly.

'I'll give you a buck fifty.'

'Well, what the hell? I'm feeling generous today. It's yours, partner,' the guy says before sipping his beer.

Just grow rhino skin and wait it out. Can't be an artist and expect anything in this world. No money, no recognition, no change in the status quo. Have to forget about all of it and just be if you want to survive. No sense in shriveling up and dying, death will come soon enough all by itself, don't you worry. Find the lush alluvial soil of your mind, plant, and harvest. Seasons will come and go like everything else. Forget the harsh reality of this physical world and keep moving. That's all there is. If you scratch beneath the surface you'll find grime.

Who knows what the hell is wrong with me? Better not even come near me, it'll only end in a fight. I don't know why, or why not. I don't know anything, just want to lie in the gutter of my own feelings and cry awhile. Nothing anybody can do about that. It isn't a crime yet, right? Doors are closing faster than before, all is becoming dark, and I am dying again. A sad bastard dying in the gutter has never been entertaining unless he gets up, dusts himself off, and marches ahead on the rails of success. Personal problems are only of value if solved by the end of the story. One man's problems are no longer the problem of the world.

Everyone is in it alone now. I've gone and made Allison sad again and now there is nothing to be done but let her be sad. I would set myself afire if it could change her mood but that would only create more problems. We have to get away from it all. Must run to the hills and start anew.

What kind of dreams will come tonight, I wonder, before I drift off to sleep? Probably be riding a Spanish mustang across the high plains. It'll be a stolen horse for I am an Apache warrior after all and require no possessions beyond my flint-edged weapons, tents, and clothing. I will ride swiftly to my hideout and eat boiled bison intestines cooked by my woman. Hope the woman in my dreams resembles Allison and wants to make it one of those memorable dreams.

We need to run to the fringes, past the fences, towards the horizon, beyond the forest, and the seas of grass. We have to leapfrog all the bullshit and find a new frontier, perhaps, settle on lush alluvial soil where we can prosper. We must not be ephemeral but persist and endure. Oh, my dear boy . . . no more thinking now . . . sleep . . . sleep . . .

# Dallas

Jesus, what the hell happened to that decade? Whatever it was, or is called, it sure did go by pretty fast, didn't it? The Zeros, was that their name, the two thousands? *The Golden Years*. It all started innocently enough for me. Hell, I had ambition and a good enough head screwed on my neck. There was work to be done too. Not much happening in music back in the early days of that mysterious decade. I wasn't listening to the radio, that's for sure. We all had high hopes for the future. Hell, it was going to be a new millennium after all. The possibilities were endless.

I got a job on a Hollywood movie that was shooting in Dallas and dropped out of art school. My old buddy Jeff and I started playing music and were trying to put a band together. That's how we met Jake and Don. They had a house out in Garland, an old suburb of Dallas. The first time Jeff and I walked in we couldn't believe our eyes. They had so many pieces of vintage gear and musical equipment you could barely walk around the place, and a record collection to die for.

They got us stoned out of our minds and played some records. 'Rare' records, as they called them.

That old vinyl changed our lives forever. Of course these days you can listen to everything on the Internet but back then you still had to know somebody and befriend them in order to have a listen. Also, nothing beats a great old tube hi-fi system when it comes to listening to music. One thing led to another and we started playing together in their house, formed a band. I moved in eventually and we had a grand old time, lived in our own little world. Took lots of mushrooms. Our band was doing pretty good too. We were starting to get a little bit of a following but the plan, as far as I saw it, was to move to New York and play with the big boys. This was before MySpace and YouTube and all that stuff, you know? Well, none of the other guys were ready to move, so I had to do it alone, but by that time the decade was already shaping up to be a bummer.

Hell, right off the bat, on my birthday, the towers go down and we're at war. I was working at a film production company owned and operated by seemingly modern and hip people but was still asked by my bosses, half seriously, if I was a terrorist. Of course once the wars started I had to listen to some of the stupidest, most misinformed, and downright cringeworthy opinions I've ever heard.

It was all becoming too much and one day when

we were doing a big commercial shoot in Mexico City, in the middle of a three-ring circus, I made up my mind to move to New York and out of cow town. A month later I was walking around Manhattan and all lay ahead. I was young and full of energy, charming even. Got myself a manager and before long was touring and signing contracts. I was playing festivals all over the place, got on the college circuit and made some good money.

The problems of the world were never far from my mind however, and that was probably what did me in, that and the drugs. The decade picked up speed and eventually got away from me completely. From 2007 to 2009 was a big blur and by 2010 everything was over for me. Hell, if you look back at that depraved decade with the wrong eyes it can blind you. How did we ever let the bastards win so completely? By the time the 2008 presidential election rolled around I knew all was being lost. Suddenly friends of mine that didn't give two shits about politics were talking about 'hope.' I kept telling them not to count on it. I was calling for a boycott of the whole electoral system.

'It will have more of an effect if we don't vote and make it known that we're not with them,' I kept saying.

'What? This guy is the real deal!' my friends kept saying.

'One man cannot change a system. He's one of them.

Who do you think is paying to get him elected? Remember Carter? He was supposedly going to change the system too.'

I had worked for the Democratic National Committee during the 2004 presidential election and knew the score. Had seen the best and brightest of the party who were assigned to run regional grassroots offices and were in charge of getting monetary contributions from people on the streets. Our people canvassing were folks looking for work as well as interested in getting Bush out of office. The guys who ran the place were all young little yuppie greedheads who were really salesmen at heart, with a degree in political science or something like that and enough hubris to drive them right to the top of the higher echelons of the Democratic party for an eventual license to steal. Or at least that's the impression I got while working for them. There were many 'strategy' meetings that resembled a scene from *Glengarry Glen Ross* and many quotas to meet. These shysters were serious about their quotas. They also ate up all of John Kerry's bullshit. Most were little more than Wall Street traders really, and I'm sure more than a few of them are roaming the hallways of our Capitol at this very moment.

I knew my friends wanted an excuse to get back to their normal lives and not be reminded of failure and wars. I knew they all just wanted to feel like they'd accomplished something by electing the right man to the highest office in the land. My friends all wanted a piece of the American Dream, or at least a last look at it even though it was dead. Well, the bastards sure did sell them good this time, I thought. Now it's all over for sure.

# New York

He's crazy about Brazil this coworker of mine. Crazy about the music, the sights, and the people. He's always sitting there at his desk and looking at photos of Brazil. When I walk in there's samba playing on the stereo. He won't go home either. Is afraid to because his next-door neighbor died and no one found out until a few days later when the smell became atrocious. One of his other neighbors put the fear into him by exclaiming 'someone's next, death is in the air' or something to that effect. He works the night shift from midnight to 8 a.m. but will not leave the office until at least eleven or noon. He is a Virgo too, same age as me, and gay. Whenever we talk about the goings-on in the world he listens and agrees but seems to think there are no avenues left for change. Thinks the world is just the way it is and that's that. I go to take the elevator to the penthouse for some coffee and Pilar, one of the janitors, asks me to hold the door. 'Sure thing,' I say.

She's got a copy of the *Times* in her hands and the front page has a picture of a few Afghans running away from gunfire on the streets of Kabul. They're all men of course and look completely terrified.

'How you say? Kaab . . . Kaa—' she says, pointing to the headline.

'Kabul,' I tell her.

'Where? This is you?'

'Me?'

'Where you from?'

'No, neighbors.'

'Oh, naiboor,' Pilar says with a smile. She told me yesterday that she is retiring this year because it takes her two hours to get to work from the Bronx. She's an old woman, will not get a raise, and her dead husband's pension will have to cover her. Maybe she can go back to Puerto Rico and live by the ocean, she says. I hope she can. As I'm pouring coffee one of the senior editors is toasting a bagel. We make eye contact and nod. I don't rush to say good morning to anybody. After a few moments he says, 'How're you doin', man?'

'Good, how're you?'

He steps away from the table. I move towards the cut fruit and notice a copy of the *Times* on one of the tables. He notices me noticing it. I shake my head. He looks at it for a moment.

'That's a great shot,' he says, referring to the photograph.

'Yeah, just wish the people in it weren't running away from explosions,' I say.

'The human condition, my man. People are just going to be killing each other one way or another.'

*Yeah? How about you just go back to your stupid pointless work and I'll go back to mine, eh fella? Keep your opinions to yourself. Keep making that big money for those big clients. Keep ramming those big advertising dollars up your ass and say 'ah'.* I call him Little John, because he's English and huge. This man who I've heard boast of Her Majesty's old empire with imperialistic nostalgia is talking to me about the human condition. I'd love to hear what he has to say about spirituality and ancient wisdom. 'The biggest empire under the sun, bar none!' he likes to say.

The coffee is the expensive kind, not very good, but strong and free. There is an assortment of goodies laid out on a table for all. We have pastries, bagels, granola, yogurt, freshly squeezed juice concoctions, vitamins, fruits, berries, and it's all free, for now. This is after all one of the premier postproduction houses in all of America. I take the elevator back down to the tenth floor where the shipping department is. This time it stops on the twelfth floor as the vice president steps in with his assistant in tow.

'What's up?' he squawks.

'Good morning,' I squawk back.

'Man, do you take the elevator down? It's a couple of flights,' he says in that beady-eyed way of his.

'Remember you asked me the same thing a few

weeks ago and I told you about my bad knee?'

'Come on, it's a couple of floors.'

'From high-school wrestling, remember?'

'You were a wrestler?' asks the assistant with a heavy dose of mistrust and a cheap jack smirk.

'Yeah, and I was pretty good too. See you, guys,' I say, exit the elevator and leave the snakes to ride down together. For these two there should be an eighth-circle-of-hell button to press in the elevator. That's where they're headed anyway. The VP is notorious for placing his bonuses above all else, human life included probably. He'll do anything to keep his position and his checks rolling in. The people who work under him are nothing to him. He's always right and if somebody doesn't like it, they're gone, doesn't matter what the circumstances. He'll screw every young girl he can screw and as of recently is on his fourth divorce. The rules don't apply to him and he'll always win. He's got the higher-ups in the palm of his hand, and the assistant, well, she puts up with it all. She aids and abets. Of course by all standards of the real world these two aren't doing anything wrong.

I walk into the shipping department where I work for my pay. There are large windows pointing south and I can see that horrible new phallic symbol creeping up towards the heavens. Billions of dollars spent building another monument to ugliness, greed, and stupidity. Why people are proud of tall structures in their cities is beyond me. They're not leading people to wisdom or a higher moral ground, they're merely more places to go to work in, if you can get it.

The shipping department is quiet and serene. The early morning rush hasn't yet begun. I turn the radio to the jazz station. What kind of a day will it be today? Come on, you heathen godless souls! Let us help and be proud of our contributions to the fall of man! 'Rejoice for the end is near,' I say into one of the security cameras.

A billionaire owns this place now, bought it a few months ago, and things are changing fast. He's one of the richest dicks in America. Whoever he sticks his shining cock into becomes a millionaire overnight, if they weren't already. He's got a golden cock, you could say. I believe he is on his fourth divorce too. Since he's bought the place his advisors are on the loose evaluating this and that. They keep gobbling up small companies to throw them all into the pot. New people show up all the time while old people disappear.

Kids barely out of college, with next to no experience in the field, are replacing older more experienced folks. Quality is going down while profits apparently soar. That's what these people are all about. They're all Mongols, they plunder, pillage, rape, and move on.

'Take the essence out, suck it dry. Real people? Who needs real people? Get some of these college kids, get rid of anybody who can expect something from us, yeah, if we have to be fair to them it'll get expensive. If they deserve something for their years of loyalty and hard work they gotta go, Jack! These college kids are already trained to take it up the rear and stab each other in the back at every turn, yeah, they're ready, throw them in, it's time for a new generation of swine!'

I try my best to breathe in this environment. There are still a few human beings left in the place and I need to eat, right? I try to be myself, try to speak the truth, try to be poetic, compassionate, rude when not treated well, not fake but real. I try to be a real human being and let the rest unfold as it may.

Allison is living with us now. I finally convinced her to move in with me and four other guys. We all moved to Bushwick, Brooklyn, to a gigantic two-story apartment. It's new and shiny, clean for now, with more space than we had before.

I am done with cocaine. 'I'll do coke again if someone can guarantee its purity. If it's uncut bring it on. I'm just sick of this shit they call cocaine. It's baking soda and baby powder,' I told the kids. So for now it's amphetamines in pill form, Alprazolam, marijuana, and booze. No more Tramadol either since I set my hair on fire on a lit candle while playing the guitar and singing for the kids. Allison liked living at the house but really wanted us to get our own place soon.

'Why don't we just buy an old VW Westfalia and travel around the county?' was my idea.

'Ha? What are you talking about?' asked Allison.

'Why not? I don't want to save our money just to hand it over to some other landlord. Why don't we get out on the road? See what we can do?'

The idea didn't exactly vibe with her but she listened.

I leave to buy some stuff for the house. Allison has made a list for me: coffee, bread, sugar, soy milk, floss, cotton balls. As soon as I leave the apartment the anxiety sets in. There are people everywhere. Mexican families, children in tow, stroll around to wherever they're not going. Yuppie couples trotting along hand in hand, thuggish-looking youngsters hanging about, old ladies with canes and walkers, decrepit-looking squatters with their dogs sitting on the sidewalk, the old man selling socks who is supposedly going to die at any moment if somebody doesn't buy something from him, delivery trucks unloading provisions, hair salons for the poor and rich alike doing good business, mangled hands and faces, muscular bodies, emaciated bodies, bodies full of life and vigor, bodies close to death, bodies born a few days ago, a few months, a few years, aging beauty queens from Patagonia, ex-villagers from the Greater Antilles, farmers from the Horn of Africa.

The whole world is walking past me. I am walking too but I might as well be standing still, not going anywhere special, just to the store for some cotton balls, coffee, and bread. The bread I will purchase is organic, homemade, local. It all used to be homemade and local when I was a child. I used to stand in line at the bakery back in Tehran. The bakers were doing all the work right in front of everyone, sweating it out right in front of the big stone ovens. Some of them used to live right above those infernal ovens. Used to take breaks sleeping on a little mattress and come down when it was their turn, wash their hands in the little sink, and get to work. Handmade, traditional, ancient, organic. Tell them how many loaves, give them the money, and walk out with bread under your arm.

The streets of Tehran back in the day (seems like a thousand years ago now) were colored in faded greens and pure blacks. Women covered in black, men in faded greens, no short sleeves, no ties, no Western influences, kill the satanic demons of the West, death to this and that, kill thought and expression, kill the child of wisdom before it grows, kill wisdom itself if you can, kill sin, murder sin like the Christians say. Murder, the sweet smell of murder, always in the air. Always mixed with sprinkled rose water, tamarind, turmeric, tea, fresh walnuts, pomegranate, lime juice, lamb's blood, goat's head, Bulgarian cheese, fresh *Barbari* bread, *Sangak* bread by the dozen, sheep sacrificed to the god of the desert rats, nomadic tribes, men of the Arabian Peninsula riding their white horses out of the scorched desert to invade the palaces. Commoners running, always running to the hills, to the caves carved in sandstone. Always counting the dead, identifying the next of kin. Always the hordes of invading crusading savages, the poetry of loss and love, of wine, of drunkenness, of the wisdom of the doomed.

Take it day by day, year by year. Centuries will pass, millennia will pass, all will pass, and evil shall perish, but the people will survive as a collective. Now all is near, it is coming, full steam ahead. The wave is starting far out in the middle of the ocean and will reach the shore soon enough. The provincial youth is forever descending his ladder from his little sweat-stained mattress to bake more bread, to pool his and his people's money together to buy the bakery, build a house, help his people move into the city, to establish a neighborhood, to speak his ethnic tongue, to fight for his bakery, his house, his family, against all, against anything and anyone who wants to take it away. I just want a few pieces of bread. My mother gave me a few coins to buy it with. She gave me a straw bag to carry it in.

I walk back home through the bazaar of human history. The Medes, the Persians, Greco-Iranians, Mongol-Iranians, Turkic Iranians, Uzbeks, Kurds,

Balochs, Arabs, Parsees. A hundred languages spoken at once. The Muslims are mourning the death of Hosein, dressed in black and gashing themselves with whips and swords. The minarets are sending out amplified death rattles. The sun is beaming through the cypress trees and the kings are forever sitting on their peacock thrones. Sometimes they have beards and sometimes they are clean shaven. They hand down edicts and proclamations, tell us about their white and red revolutions, say they are our fathers. I keep walking, a child with bread to take home to his family. My mother will be happy to see me, my father is off fighting the thousand-year war.

Allison is in the shower when I walk in, will be out any moment and reveal her divine wet body. Water will be dripping from her as she walks to the bedroom to cast her towel aside and stand there in pure naked glory. She will put on her shea butter, blow-dry her hair, put on her make-up, dress, and leave for work. She will be happy to have me in her life and smile and say, 'I love you.' She will leave and I will be here alone with my thoughts.

*Alone with the memory of my genes, my past lives. Many lives lived between the great rivers, the fertile crescent, the Persian Steppes, the Iranian Plateau, coastal plains of the Gulf of Persia, coastal forests of the Caspian, herding my sheep, fighting for the kings, toiling in the fields, sharpening tools, plowing, sowing seeds, listening to the wind sweeping over Dasht-e Kavir, in the shadow of Yazd's Tower of Silence, running with the Caspian Tiger's ghost, running from the Mongolian hordes, running from all that comes to pass.*

# Europe

My mother and father live in the flatlands of north Texas. At the end of the Great Plains, where the winds come down from what man has called Canada. They toil in the imaginary fields of their minds. How I remember them walking hand in hand on the rooftop of our little apartment building in Tehran while they planned their escape from the clutches of the Islamic regime and imagined a brighter future.

'If we go to Turkey and try the German embassy . . . We can go to France and stay with your brother! How about Belgium?' I remember my mother saying.

You could see the blue dome of some important mosque in the distance among many other buildings; behind everything the ever-present Alborz Mountains marked the city's natural boundaries. That ruthless demon king, devil-faced, cockroach fucker Khomeini had died a few months before and by the time we got to Germany the Berlin Wall was coming down. Millions of people in the streets shouting this and that all over the place, believing that something was changing, or that an era had come to an end and another was beginning.

My father had been kicked out of the Air Force after eight years of fighting, for being against the regime, and was driving an old minibus around for money, and lucky to be alive. We sold everything and bought visas. We had to escape and become refugees, to get asylum somewhere. We had family in France, took a plane to Rome, Alitalia flight something or other. I looked down at Tehran for the last time as the plane ascended. We paid an astronomically high price for salami sandwiches at Aeroporto Leonardo da Vinci di Fiumicino, '*signore e signori*,' that's all I can remember them saying on the loudspeakers. Took a night plane to Paris Charles de Gaulle airport, got picked up by my uncle, who had escaped the regime in the early days, and everyone was happy to be together. I slept in the hallway on a little mattress.

When I wake up my first assignment is to get bread.

'All you have to say is *une baguette, s'il vous plaît,* got it?' one of my cousins says to me.

*Une baguette, s'il vous plaît. Une baguette, s'il vous plaît.*

I go down to the corner store for *une baguette.* What

a difference in color, themes, all is cheerful and alive, everyone seems free and happy, all is bright blues, bright greens, and cheerful reds. I decide to throw in a *bonjour* of my own before the *une baguette, s'il vous plaît*. It works like a charm. *Merci! Au revoir!*

*Au revoir*, yes, sweet, sweet *au revoir* to all that came before, my eleven-year-old brain is thinking, this is where we shall make a home at last. From one baguette to *Qu'ils mangent de la brioche!* I will learn it all, will become French and run around in short pants and a scarf around my neck asking everyone I see about bread and cakes, poetry, democracy, and revolution. I will sing in French, kiss in French, travel to the provinces and see it all for myself, will join a circus, will dance and sing!

Standing there in front of the Arc de Triomphe my uncle leans down and gives me some historical background, tells me about Hitler and his army who marched down Champs Élysées after the fall of France, and my heart skips a few beats. I can see them in black and white. We leave France two days later. Goodbye, French self, goodbye, *une baguette, bonne nuit, c'est la vie*. There is no European Union just yet and we have to sneak across the border to Belgium, where another uncle picks us up. Now we are in the land of the Flemish. I find the language to be unmelodious, to say the least. They don't live in Brussels or Antwerp but in a little village somewhere.

'Beautiful countryside!' my uncle declares before giving my parents a rundown of the asylum deal they can expect. My mother hates it, can't see herself in a village, she's a big-city girl after all. I don't mind it so much, it's small and quaint, the streets are not threatening with riot, fire, violence. I can envision a quiet life here, one of study, of socialistic advancement. Here one has to learn three languages right off the bat! I can do that! I'd love to learn them, and Latin too. Wow! Sounds great, let's do it. Let's become Belgian then, why not? Nothing doing, we leave after a few days. My uncle takes us to the border of Germany, where we walk through a small patch of jungle and sneak across.

On the other side my aunt's husband picks us up in his little VW Golf, we don't have that much with us, just a few suitcases, so we all pile in and ride to Charlemagne's old capital, the city known for its hot sulfur springs, where many a Germanic king was crowned amongst the cold medieval architecture, the city of Aachen. The Berlin Wall is coming down a few hundred miles to the east. The immigrant houses are waiting for us. My mother feels at home with her sisters here, we are staying, I must learn the lay of the land. *Guten Morgen . . . Brötchen bitte?*

Soon they'll tire of us here and we'll tire of them. It will be time to pack up and keep it moving but only right after we're beginning to feel comfortable, only when friendships have formed, only after gaining a small foothold, only when the language is starting to make sense. Soon it will be JFK airport in the dead of summer to catch a connecting flight to DFW airport. Soon it will be another aunt picking us up. Soon we will see the depleted grasslands of north Texas. A voice is echoing, 'Here, boy, is where you'll come to grow into a man. Who'd a thunk it, ha?'

Has the past ever been so dead and alive at the same time? There was nothing to say before and there is even less to say now. There is no point in speaking to most people: they simply don't understand. There is no point in feeling bad about that. It means nothing. Makes no difference at all.

What does it take for one to disconnect? Is that even a possibility? Aren't we all supposed to be responsible? Can we just disconnect? How do you cut ties with the human race? Not in reality, only in visions and dreams, right? In reality one is and stays connected, not only to the human race of the present, but the human race eternal, the ones who came before and the ones who will come after. The spirits fly, energy flows.

'The dandelions in spring sure do look defeated and worn,' I speak to my image in the mirror. I don't know what that means or why I said it. Sometimes I say things that don't mean anything at the time they are spoken but take on some kind of meaning later on. I do that in song too.

You can be right, right to the grave. I never thought I'd be around virgins again, these young girls hanging around our house, coming and going at all hours. Not that it means anything to me. It just feels strange hearing so-and-so is a virgin. There are four or five of them and I think at least three were virgins when they started coming around. Now it seems there's only one with her flower intact, as it were. I've barely said a serious word to any of them. Got no reason to say anything besides hello and goodbye. I got a woman and there ain't any other gonna take me away, and that's really besides the point anyway. I'm not their older brother, uncle, or father even. I got nothing to say to them little girls and I don't want any trouble, you see. The way they jump from guy to guy in our little group is funny in a not so funny kind of way. Our little group . . . I can't believe I'm hanging out with these young fellas. If it wasn't for the music we play together I'd probably be somewhere far away.

Hard drugs on a regular basis can make for a foggy existence and make one say, 'Wow! That was already a year and a half ago?' Yes, it sure as hell was. Oh the illusion of sped-up time. It's not going by faster, fella, you're just not remembering as much because frankly you don't want to remember all the crazy stuff you did while coked-up and drunk out of your mind. Allison and I will be moving this weekend to build our own private love nest.

This is the land of monumental egos but monumental egos are nothing new in the history of mankind. The ancient tribes have seen many come and go but more are always on their way. Looking in the mirror I can see more lines in my face, more gray hairs, but the eyes are still glowing. Will no one give this immigrant a chance? They say if you want power, you've got to take power. Well, I don't want to take it, don't want the kind of power that needs to be attained and protected with force. Real power is something entirely different. A mountain has real power, a sea, the sun.

Got a lot of hours to go . . . goddamn, how am I gonna do it with these stupid people all around me, asking this 'n' that? I think I'm gonna piss in the corner and walk out, spitting on a few of them. Sure wish I could, but I've been civilized and condemned. If I had an ounce of decency left I'd do it, but as I've said many times in the past, you've got to pay the rent.

Those treacherous genes of mine, if only they could surface and annihilate the good genes, run amok and paint the walls in blood, not my blood, not their blood.

As it stands now the only blood I can spill is metaphorical blood. My blood's too red for spilling. It's deep crimson. There isn't really a word for it in English, or Persian, or French. There was a word for it back before there wasn't a word for word, back when we all just grunted at each other but knew exactly what the grunts meant.

# New York

I played Lou Reed's *Berlin* for about thirty minutes until it got too personal. You know, introspective lyrics that really hit home and bring tears to the eyes while you're sitting around co-workers. That's not my kind of scene. I prefer to cry alone. So I asked Larry if he had his iPod with him today and he said yes and put on some Beach Boys. Goddamn silly putty watered-down rock 'n' roll. I don't give a shit about it. I mean it sounds nice enough most of the time recording-wise and the performances are amazing, but come on. I'm a grown man. I can't be listening to this teenybopper crap all day long. I need some serious stuff, but then again maybe all this seriousness is killing me.

It's really all about getting through the day, the week, or month as far as the job is concerned. Luckily I can shake it off most days, but other days it's harder. Everywhere you look somebody's saying, 'You want this done? Well, I'm your man!' Somebody's willing to put in the overtime, if not for the time and a half, then for the advancement opportunities. Smiling real wide, small-talking, whatever it takes. All day long, nights and weekends. No vacation, no rest, no life.

How can I get through the day today? How can I work with these people who don't care about anything but the things that don't count? How can I keep resisting the urge to flee? Not that there is anywhere to go. I work for a billionaire who sits atop his golden mountain. Below him sit a few millionaires and below them some others who want to be sitting on millions. These people took away our names and gave us numbers but nobody complained. Nobody said a word except for me. Nobody even asked why. I just wanted to hear it from one of their lackey's mouths. I knew why, but just wanted to hear it, you know? Of course they did it for us. For efficiency and us. For me! They gave me a number for my sake.

These people I work with, most of them are normal everyday people, you know. They don't ask any questions. Just do what needs to be done and never complain. To be uncooperative is the ultimate sin in the workplace. It is a crime to hold up the line and ask a simple question like, Why are we doing this? You've got to be a professional. You got to take it up the rear and like it. If you take it good and hard then one day it could be, it just could be your turn to stick it to somebody else. But you better do your best to belong, boy. You better not stick out.

Trying to remember my genetic memory. Trying to

unplug. The air isn't clean. Too many synthetic waves pollute the knowledge floating around. Trying to remember my genetic memory.

'Do you know what I can make on a five grand investment?' says my high-school friend who is now a millionaire to me over the telephone.

'Yeah, yeah, I'm sure you can get a lot, but this isn't an ordinary investment, this is art,' I say, trying to sell him on the idea of putting on a play of mine in Brooklyn – but he'll have none of it, wouldn't give me a penny if I begged him. The play is a real scorcher, but what the hell. I feel like a trapped animal of some kind. I don't know what kind of an animal. It's not so complicated a thing to feel trapped in this godforsaken city.

'Lots of good churches up there in New York, buddy,' my old friend Jeff said to me over the phone the other day.

'You see, Jeff,' I told him, 'it's the thing that makes the thing do the thing that it does, to become the thing that's really the thing, you know?'

'What are you talking about now, you crazy bastard?' he says to me, my old friend Jeff, God-loving Jeff, friend of Jesus Jeff, Jeff the mighty dynamo doing the Lord's work and not ever resting. He's got a radio show now along with his real-estate business, talks about money and mortgages, and makes a good living. We used to be in a band together in the good old days, when all lay frontwards and glowed in the night, before the countless calamities, mishaps, and mistaken identities, when we were true believers and fearless. In those golden years of twine and wood, of shipbuilding, of tomorrows without regret, no rue, rebuild it when it falls, wind in the hair and face, smell of the ocean far away, the sun above, every blade of grass perfectly placed, moving forward, always forward.

'Nothing,' I say, 'I'm not talking about anything. Well, I am, but it can wait. What I really wanted to tell you is that I finally believe in the resurrection, not the way you do, you fat bastard, but in my own peculiar way.'

'Well! Hey, man, that's great, wow, brother!'

'Yeah, but please for the love of God don't give me any of your sermons now. I just listened to your forlorn radio show on the Internet, isn't that enough?'

'Ha! Did you like it?'

'Well, sure. You did well, for a third-rate regional radio personality, yeah, hell, *real* well! I guess it's good information for homeowners and people of that ilk but, eh, for me, well, you know . . .'

'Yeah, I know. When are you coming to Dallas?'

'Soon, gotta see my sister's kid, you know? How's your wife?'

'Good, we're good. You know I own my own branch now, right?'

'Yeah? Well, congratulations, buddy, don't get too rich now! Remember the camel and the needle's eye.'

'Ha! Right! God's been working on you, buddy, I'm gonna say a prayer for you today.'

'Well, God bless you, friend, and while you're at it say a prayer for us all,' I say.

'Will do, listen, I'm gonna be up there in a few weeks for a radio conference, would love to see you, man.'

'What! That's great, buddy! Why didn't you say so?'

'Because you won't give me a second to speak, you dirty bastard. Will you be around?'

'Of course I'll be around. If you need to stay with Allison and me we'd love to have you.'

'Oh, thanks, man. I'll be at a hotel, Linda's not coming with. I've got some business up there too.'

'Business, ha? Okay, well you let me know when you're up here.'

I haven't seen Jeff for a couple of years now. Last time I saw him he was in a world of trouble with his marriage and business, but eventually everything worked itself out I guess, and he's back on the rails of success. He's one of a handful of real friends I have left in this world. Friends who will hide you inside their homes and hear your side of the story before calling the cops. Friends who will hand you all the money in their wallet and say, 'Here, take this, that's all the cash I have at the house . . . and take the keys to the car, I'll report it stolen in the morning, that'll give you plenty of time to get out of the state.' Friends who will come to your aid and who you'll help in turn, who will speak of what's in their hearts with abandon. Who will speak the truth and tell you what they think of you. Well, Jeff was that kind of a friend to me. I just always wished he could have stuck with music, but to each his own.

I decided to call in sick to work this morning, why the hell not? Been trying to get a raise for the last three months and the damn vice president keeps avoiding me. We're only talking about a couple of bucks here, nothing crazy, just a decent wage for a decent man. He must still be pissed off about that email I sent out condemning our company for doing that commercial for a giant agricultural biotechnology corporation. Allison has gone to the park. I think I'll go to the cemetery. Something must be done here. An era is ending and another needs to begin. I don't like stagnation. I had spoken to Allison again about leaving.

'I'll quit my job or try to get laid off,' I told her.

'What? Then what?' she asked.

'Then we go on the road. We'll work on organic farms and talk to the people who work with the land, to ah . . . we'll visit Native American reservations and see if there's anything we can do. It'll probably be dangerous but what the hell? I've stayed in New York too long, babe, need to talk to some other kinds of people. I know you're younger and haven't lived here as long . . .'

'Being younger has nothing to do with it, I just want to plan things out a little better. You just want to go and figure things out later.'

'Yeah, improvising! I like improvising.'

'Well, let's just think it through more, let's brainstorm.'

She was right of course but I wish there was a way to speed up the process. I really wanted to go and talk to people who work the land, see if they could teach me a little something. In New York it's all about competition, people getting off the boat and immediately staking a claim.

Walking around the cemetery I can't help but laugh at some of these jackasses with their mausoleums and obelisks. Some of the tombs are as large as subway entrances, like the one on 72nd Street and Broadway, Atlantic Avenue, or something like that. Some graves have gigantic statues of the deceased, or of a female crying on their tombstone. Let it go, you fools. Just think what else could have been done with that money, how many families could have been fed and clothed.

Walking around the cemetery you see the same famous names that streets are named after, subway stops, schools . . . these goddamned frightened fools and their legacies, how afraid of dying they were, how intent on keeping a name alive as if the name is where all knowledge and wisdom are contained. Around the dead graves exists the most abundant life, trees, birds, water lilies, fish, frogs, insects. I suppose this place would be a parking lot if it weren't for the graves but it's still funny to see pomposity in action.

I got the same feeling walking around Washington DC once. I had some time to kill on this particular trip and went to as many national historic sites as I could. I went to the National Mall, Lincoln Memorial, Vietnam War Memorial, and finally decided to go to Arlington National Cemetery and pay my respects to the martyrs. I walked around and said my own kind of prayer for the dead soldiers' souls, thanked them, then walked up to Arlington House, which was Robert E. Lee's old residence and overlooks the Potomac river. From up there one can see the real layout of the capital and the power it displays. Not spiritual power, but a dominating power, an enslaving power. All the monuments are white and unnatural-looking sticking out of the green landscape. All is spread out, spread apart, un-united-looking. I notice very little difference between those obelisks, statues, and mausoleums and these here in this cemetery where I'm now walking. Both were built for the dead, not the living. But don't take my word for it, friend, go and see it for yourself.

Driving across this magnificently beautiful land of ours one wonders why everything is fenced off and owned by unseen masters. One wonders why the people can't farm upon the land and share their bounty with one another, why we don't have the right or the time to think and talk out there, why we can't solve our own problems out here in the open? The masters told the natives, 'We are your fathers.' I have two fathers, one of them is the sun, and the other never claims to own me.

'Jeff,' I say as we're sitting in a restaurant, 'remember when we were in New Orleans that one time and you talked about our generation not being ready for the keys to the city?'

'Yeah,' he says while staring out the window, where crowds of people are walking about on East Houston Street.

'Well, I'm ready. Are you?'

'What do you mean?' he asks while taking a sip of Scotch.

'Why don't we go into business together?'

'What kind of business?'

'Feeding people for free, putting people to work, from city to city, county to county. The idea I was telling you about? That kind of business.'

'Sure, it's a great idea. I don't know if I'd call that a business but . . . Why don't you put an ad online or something, see who's interested?' Jeff says.

'No, that's not the way to do it. I don't want to start it in New York. Don't want go-getters and fast-talker, mover-shaker types. I want to start out in the middle of the country, out west somewhere, where the soil is clean and the people communicate slower.'

'Okay, hmmm . . .'

'See, we've got to recruit our army from places near rivers and streams, near hills and mountains, where the air is clean and stars visible at night.'

'Our army, eh, you crazy bastard?'

'Yeah, through observation and learning, through speech and thought, clear and coherent thought ripened by time, not by some clock! Then we'll ride into town on a donkey and put on a real show for them!'

'Do it, sounds good to me,' he says while looking away.

'Good, then give me some money,' I say while sticking out the palm of my hand.

'What?'

'Yeah, you've got the money and I've got the time. Allison and I'll drive across the country and learn from the best. We'll set it all up. There'll be no monetary rewards for any of us. It's an adventure.'

'You think you'll have the courage to go through with it?' he asks.

'I don't know, but I'd like to find out.'

'Ah, with my money?'

'Yes, it'll take courage on all sides! We are men, right? And this is America, isn't it? Where the hell is our pioneering spirit? You want to wait for the politicians to fix it? Or will it be the bastards working in finance? Advertising? No, friend, it has to be the real people, the crazy people. No blogs, no videos, just doing what needs to be done under the radar. It'll build and build the old-fashioned way. I don't care about faster. Fast is not what we want in the beginning. We're starting at the beginning and need to observe and learn before we move forward.'

'Aha, okay. So, how much do you need?' he says, trying to speed up the inevitable.

'Let's start with five grand.'

'Jeez . . .'

'If you tell me about what you can do with a five grand investment I'll rip out your spleen and burn it on the bar, or not, because I'm a peaceful soul and you're much bigger than me, but I'll never speak to you again.'

'What, you just want me to hand over five grand and not ask any questions?'

'No, ask all the questions you want, but if you don't ask the right questions it'll be useless. Remember all those stories about contracts on paper napkins? Deals made with a handshake? What happened to that?'

He said he'd think it over and discuss it with his wife, admitted it would be a tremendous undertaking, said it would be biblical, and I agreed. I found it hard to sleep that night, would wake up every hour and look over at Allison sleeping beside me. Will she go along with me? I kept thinking. What if Jeff doesn't give me any money? One has to act alone sometimes but how glorious it is to have help.

We have to go, have to keep moving. Must not let the spirit die. This is our country and we are free to walk upon it. We are free to talk, free to think, free to ask, free to say. Free if we want to be.

# On the Road

I was getting drunker and the city was getting to me in a bad way. Something was going to give in the frightful night stream. The path forward was clogged up, tangled and twisted with a torrent of unknowns and hollowed-out confidences. You are dealing with a flawed man: forgive me and love me, I say to all and sundry.

It was under flashing strobes, red lights, smoke, and screams that we assembled as a group once more. It was New Year's Eve and Allison was gone. Dari was back and so were a lot of others. I was in a band again, with the kids. The fantastic lights were calling and there was no way out, except for a sort of death. My baby was gone for now, we wounded each other beyond repair. She needed to go. Sweet Allison needed to go home to Florida and start anew. Jeff and his wife decided not to give us any money.

We were once again going on a cross-country tour. Kiarash, the drummer of our band, is the newest member to make it out of Iran and now lives with the kids. He and I had one of those instant bonds that develop between people who are supposed to ride down the road a while together. He's tall and handsome, with deep, dark eyes. The girls go nuts for him. 'Stay as long as you need to,' he told me.

We have to gather all the necessary supplies for the first leg of the tour. In our case the provisions consist mostly of drugs. Bottles of amphetamine, synthetic opiates, hydrocodone, and an ounce of marijuana, which all have to be procured before departure and it's early afternoon before we point the van plus trailer towards the western shores. I let the manager drive first and we're off, first over the Verrazano Bridge flying over the narrows where one can catch a glimpse of an imaginary Europe with a deep stare to the east, then through New Jersey, where the first of many portents to come awaits before nightfall. The natural marvel of which I speak is the Delaware Water Gap with its Silurian sandstone magnificence, Mount Tammany and Mount Minsi longingly staring at one another from either side of the Delaware river, which has cut so skillfully through the Appalachian ridge.

The deciduous forests cloaking the slopes and valleys of Pennsylvania will soon be waking from their winter slumber to sprout forth with the most delightful colors imaginable, but for now a barren cold loneliness shrouds all things. Nightfall comes hard and fast, now it's my turn to drive and I take the wheel after a quick stop for gas and food. My thoughts are speedy from the speed and I'm seeing shadows and apparitions. My mind is on Allison and ghosts of the Lenni-Lenapi. I can see their ancient fires burning through openings in the rows of oaks, hickories, maples, and ash. I see wild horses and packs of hungry wolves chasing them. I hear drums and chants.

Sundown, then dawn breaks again. Constant vehicular motion, clear but cold, everything's fine. Loons zooming across a white landscape. Screams and smoke. Some are up and some are down. Snow-covered fields and prevailing northeasterly winds. White on white on white, we drove through the day and through the night. San Francisco's visible but another two days' drive from where we last stopped for gas.

Daytime again, heavy snow and icy roads, lunch at a diner, blue eyes laughing. Another day and night of driving with the wind a constant menacing companion, then it all clears up again.

And every time I take the wheel my mind starts to wander and comb through the recent past with my sweet gone Allison and wonders what went wrong. Was it doomed from the rocky, smoky, speedy, boozy start in that dark stinking loft? Or was it our last apartment and toothless Frank from the basement with his whooping death cough who brought us warped warty vegetables from the garden, or the lowlife landlord with his indecipherable rotten

English in that graveyard neighborhood? Was it her waitress job or her cracked frontal lobe? Was it my drinking and drugging, my burning with ancient guilt and fright? I get no answers, only more questions, until the speed starts to overtake me and my soul races ahead faster than the speeding van plus trailer, circles the Earth and shoots out towards Mercury, my ruling planet. Somebody screams something in the back and brings me out of my head to pretend everything's okay when it isn't.

I want to turn the van around and point it towards Tallahassee.

At a rest area now, after a long piss I walk around behind the building with the bathroom in it. I focus my eyes on the darkness and suddenly see a mind-blowing scene. I'm standing in front of the Great Salt Flats in the dark. I've been here before, not to this exact spot but close. I was with her, June, the green-eyed one from long ago, and we were driving from Texas to California by way of Oklahoma, her red convertible two-door hitched to the back of our rented U-Haul truck. We were both nineteen and on our way to test our mettle in LA with the rest of the dreamers in the last years of the twentieth century. It would take us three days to reach LA. Our first stop was Sayre, Oklahoma, to visit her grannies. Grandma Marge and Grandma Annie, one was the mother of the other. Sayre is a small town, Route 66 used to run through it and John Ford filmed some scenes there for *The Grapes of Wrath*.

June, the girl I speak of, tried to pass me off as a friend and I had to go along with the story and sleep in another room to keep up appearances. I think the grannies knew the score, they were smart ole cookies who made their money in the natural gas boom and basically owned the whole town. 'Man-eaters,' according to June. They lived in a gigantic house on a large piece of land with horses and dogs. I didn't ask June why she passed me off as a friend and couldn't care less about the racial undertones of her decision. All I cared about was doing the deed with her as many times as I could for as long as I could, all else be damned.

She was such a hot piece of ass that guys would run up to her everywhere we went and try to pick her up, didn't matter if I was around or not. We'd be in a mall, or at a movie, or just walking down the street. One time we were stopped at a light in her red-hot convertible and a dude got out of his car, ran up, and threw in a crumpled piece of paper with his number on it then got back in his car before the light turned. None of that bothered me, on the contrary I got a kick out of it. After all I was the one on top of her every day and night. Hell, I even got her pregnant once. She did have a habit of sleeping around on me now and then but I just turned around and did the same to her and all was peachy.

The first time I saw her we were both juniors in high school. The crowd parted and there she stood in the middle of the hallway with her friend Frenchy. June was the most angelic thing I'd ever laid eyes on, long exquisite golden locks, lovely white skin, a radiant smile, luscious curves, and a feisty disposition. She looked like a young Cybill Shepherd but with green eyes instead of blue. I only got to talk to her once then her mother sent her away to military school because her and Frenchy were cokeheads, and I didn't get to see her again until our second year of college. She had a boyfriend then but I managed to steal her away somehow.

Anyway, we were driving to LA and after visiting with her cool ole grannies went to see her father in Amarillo, in the Texas panhandle. Her daddy had fallen in love with his secretary and left June's man-eating momma when June was six, word was that he could've been rich if he'd just played along but he'd had enough of June's mother and left to find happiness instead of riches. The old man was a nice enough dude, tall, stoic, and handsome, with two other daughters almost as pretty as June. He didn't buy the friend bit at all because he was a smart cookie too, but took a liking to me anyway. We stayed at his house for an hour or so, drank iced tea, then were off again, stopped outside of Amarillo on I-40 and got it on. Just pulled over on the shoulder and got down to it. She liked to ride me in cars. At night when it was time to get a hotel

June told the front desk woman the room was for her alone and that I was a friend from around that part of the country, just helping her with her bags, and only staying for an hour. The next morning she got charged for two occupants.

'"Excuse me but there seems to be some kind of mistake," I told her,' June was telling me as we drove along the highway, her long lustrous blond hair blowing in the wind while she was looking at me through her Audrey Hepburn sunglasses, feet propped up on the dash, and drinking a Dr. Pepper through a straw.

'The woman goes, "There's no mistake, miss, we heard you guys all night long and know that your 'friend' never left!"' she said, laughing joyously like a child after the punchline.

I got a kick out of that. I used to make her sing like a bird in those days, loved hearing her scream my name in that Texas/Oklahoma drawl of hers. 'Ooh . . . baby . . . Ahhh . . . Aali, Aaliii . . . Aaalliii!'

She was my blond green-eyed dream girl and I never could get enough. The second night of the trip we stopped in Flagstaff, Arizona, and although it was the middle of July the air was cool and crisp. We went walking among the ponderosa pines holding hands and looking at each other with adoring eyes, made love in a nice old hotel overlooking downtown then took off early the next morning. At every truck stop along our route there were eyes on us, envious eyes.

We got to LA around ten o'clock at night on the third day and went to the house June had arranged for us to rent. It was on Ventura Boulevard in Studio City, right under the hill, a five-bedroom with four others living there, all of whom worked in film production or at an agency of some kind. It was glorious for the first couple of months because we had a little money saved up and didn't have to find a job right off, used to stay home and do it five or six times a day.

We'd drive around in her little car and dream of the star-filled nights of our future with the wind in our hair. We'd go down to the beach and lie around without a care in the world. Used to visit porn shops and do it in the little booths or go to the mall and do it in the dressing rooms. She was a wild girl, liked to do it in public places. We even drove to Tijuana one night, how I had the balls to walk around with her down there, I'll never know. We met a group of young Mexicans and hung around with them, got so drunk on tequila I could barely drive back, and to make it harder June was going down on me most of the way.

It all turned ugly soon enough though, neither of us found a job for a long time and our money ran out. Her grannies sent her some dough but that ran out too after a while so we had to move out of the dream house and into a crummy little apartment in Van Nuys, where June worked as an assistant property manager for some lowlife little pimp bastard. She used to sneak me into the back office and give me a treat every now and then, push me down on her chair behind the desk, slide off her panties, hike up her skirt and sit on my rock-hard manhood while I pulled her long blond hair from the back and let her bite the back of my hand to keep from screaming.

There was a pool in the middle of that ragged apartment building and one time we went down there around midnight and June stripped off her clothes and did her best Marilyn Monroe act from that doomed last movie with Dean Martin. I jumped in after her, caught up to her on the steps, and let her bite the back of my hand again. Her pimp bastard of a boss's apartment overlooked the pool and I think he caught a glimpse of our performance.

I got a job working retail of all things, used to see movie stars all the time. After a while June found an agent and started hanging out with producers, directors, and older actor types. She'd take me along at first but I could see that these dudes wanted to be alone with her and I was fully aware of how Hollywood worked, so I'd stay behind and let her stick her hooks in them.

Back in Dallas, before we left, all was dreamy. Thinking back on it now, it was one of the best times of my life. I had good friends, was going to college studying theater, it was a nationally recognized award-winning program too, and garnered me scholarships to several universities around the country. I was a crowd favorite and besides being an okay actor was cast in plays because at least a hundred or more people would show up during the two-week run just to see me. My corner of the dressing room was always filled with flowers from adoring fans and friends after every performance. I knew scores of people back then. The theater director sat me down one day and assured me I'd be able to go to Juilliard if I stayed with him another year. I was in peak physical form, looked like a damn Greek statue, worked for my father in that great little Italian restaurant he was part-owner of, and made decent money. I shared an apartment with two of the best girls in our theater troupe, had a great little car and what have you.

June worked as a cocktail waitress at a strip club in those days, used to make three to five hundred bucks a night. One time she came to my apartment after work at four in the morning screaming and dragged me downstairs to show what some guy had tipped her. It was a brand new Porsche 911 convertible with the title and everything. The bastard had even given her three hundred extra bucks for her first speeding ticket.

'Well hell, baby, let's go for a ride,' I said and got behind the wheel, and we went speeding around town until the sun came up, parked it behind an office building, and she jumped on me like she loved to do. We had to give the thing back though because the next morning we let a couple of buddies of mine drive it around and they came back with a box they'd found in the trunk which contained among other things some random photos of people at a birthday party, a pair of black gloves, and a .22 pistol with a box of ammo.

'The gun works fine, we did a little target practice in the field behind Spring Creek,' my buddy informed us. One of my roommates, Sally, had a cop friend and we asked her to ask him for a little background on the generous tipper. The cop said the tipper had a daughter the same age as June. He thought something smelled fishy. Shit, I had already gotten one of my rich friends' daddies who was a doctor to agree to buy the damn thing at fifteen grand under the value of the car, since that model was brand new and hard to find. The doctor daddy would have given us cash no questions asked, but it was just too damn risky, said June. We kept the pistol though and took it to LA with us.

'Don't you wonder what she had to do to get that car, Ali?' Sally asked me at some point.

'I don't care, Sally, I don't care what she had to do. She can do what she wants, you see?' I shot back at her.

'Hmm . . . I'd be really careful if I were you. She's a liar. Don't move to LA with her. Stay here with us. Don't go with her.'

'I'm going with her and I love her. I know who she is and what she does, and you know what? I don't care, she's worth it and she's mine.'

Sally and I had gotten it on a few times when June was on holiday with her mother and were quite fond of one another. Sally had a tongue six inches long and was the craziest girl I've ever had in the sack. I did all I could to satisfy her but one or two orgasms just weren't enough and she'd go on without me after I was done. That damn girl would get herself off three or four more times with me lying there beside her and not even pay attention to me. Hell, one time I got up and went back to my room and she didn't even notice, just kept stroking her magnificent middle. Sally died in a car crash while I was in LA and I didn't even make it to her funeral. She was so beautiful and talented, God rest her soul.

Things were great in those days. We were teenagers and the whole world was ours but for some reason none of that was enough for me and I decided to take the short cut to stardom instead of a calculated academic-based crawl. Who knows, maybe it was June's incredible vagina that started me down that adventurous path? She ended up leaving me after about six months in LA. I was visiting my parents in Dallas and didn't hear from her the last two nights I was there. When I got to LA I found out she was staying with somebody else, some actor in his late twenties. They came and picked up her stuff a few days after I landed. I pretended to be cool, shook the dude's hand, smiled at them both, told June to let me know if she needed anything, but dropped to the floor as soon as they left and the door closed to cry my eyes out. I never asked her why she left, had too much pride for a thing like that.

# Los Angeles

I started hanging out with a guy named Jessie, an older actor who was the brother of a theater buddy of mine from Dallas. We spent the next couple of months drinking like madmen. I wasn't even old enough to walk into a bar yet but he managed to sneak me in or else would buy us a bottle of booze and we'd get drunk at home and talk about New York, how much he loved it when he used to live there and how sure he was that one day I'd call it home.

'You're made for New York!' Jessie would say. 'Do yourself a favor, my boy, and move your little crying ass there immediately, find yourself a model girlfriend and try to do some good theater, forget this shit out here. I mean, what kind of roles are you gonna get? Even if you get lucky you'll be playing terrorists for the next twenty years. Is that what you want? Go to New York, my boy, and be a real actor! On stage, sonny! That's where you prove yourself, on stage!'

We'd go up and down Hollywood looking for trouble, and would find it too. Jessie knew lots of seedy characters, mostly dope fiends and sluts but colorful nevertheless. We'd get stoned and drunk then bum around Melrose or Sunset to see what we could pick up, and if nothing happened go to one of his slutty girlfriend's houses so he could get his fill. I was too heartbroken to do too much but sometimes I wasn't so heartbroken and did some things.

We'd sway with the wind and there was no telling where we'd end up on any given night. Then he landed a movie gig in New York and left.

'I'll be seeing you in the Big Apple, my boy; as soon as this stupid movie wraps I'll land a play, I can feel it. The stage, my boy, the stage! So stay in touch.'

After a month or so of bumming around on my own I got some kind of virus and became really sick, so sick that I had to take myself to a free hospital and wait almost a day to be seen by a doctor who told me to rest as much as possible and take my pills. It was the end of the line for me in LA so I bought myself a bus ticket.

I don't remember much about the bus ride back to Dallas, only that the last two hundred miles of it was in an historic Texas thunderstorm with tornados touching down all around us and the sky lit up with lightning, hellfire, and doom.

Back in Dallas I got a job working in a bank and started to go to art school. My father thought I could learn to become a camera operator and work for CNN or something but I just knew I was going to be the next Elia Kazan or perhaps a Bob Rafelson. I made it for about a semester without getting into trouble then on my twenty-first birthday my best friend Ardeshir took me to this club his new friends owned and I took MDMA with these two floozies for the first time and that was that.

Around the same time I met a tall, skinny, crazy southern girl at school who already had a boyfriend but took a liking to me. Monika was her name and her face was too magical for words: high cheekbones, honey-brown eyes, perfectly full and luscious cracked lips, and the most incredibly soft skin I've ever touched. She was a sensational painter too, with the most far-out taste in music. She'd make me compilation cassette tapes and give them to me in front of her boyfriend. Monika and I used to stay up all night at her aunt's house and get into all kinds of stuff when the boyfriend wasn't around. She was a pill popper of the highest order and also the first girl who made me feel beautiful. She'd wash me in a warm bath when my prick wasn't working because of the drugs, hold my face in her hands, and tell me I was beautiful. That had a magical effect on my prick. Afterwards she'd often lie beside me and talk about Mondrian and Kandinsky.

Around that time I started working at the nightclub Ardeshir's friends owned. I did the lights and danced, three times a night, in a cage suspended above the dance floor, wearing an alien costume. I was pretty popular on the scene and Monika would come by when her boyfriend wasn't around to hang out. She was impressed by my club connections, I could get her in and always had free drugs. I was absolutely and completely in love with her but then she entered a contest, got discovered by an agent, and signed a modeling contract in New York. A month or two later she was gone. Next time I heard from her she was divorced from her older photographer husband and going to rehab.

June and I would see each other every year for the next five after she left me and no matter who we were with at the time always managed to sneak a good hour or two in somewhere. Last time I saw her was right before I moved to New York ten years ago. She had a successful wine-selling business, wanted me to marry her and move to Austin, but I was New York-bound with dreams of my own. Last time I talked to her was five years ago when I called her on a whim while snorting heroin in a crummy Queens apartment. She said she was married and that her father and one of her grannies had died but that her mother was alive and remarried.

## On the Road (Again)

Monika is married too now. All these memories are ricocheting around my cranium as I drive across this beautiful country, state after state, mile after mile. I've been to all these places before, with memories attached to every corner of this land. Every time I take the wheel my mind drifts towards the past, must be the speed, or something trying to tell me something. Every woman in my life has either left me or been left by me.

I zip us through Nevada and into California the next day. The air changes and we can breathe again. Sunshine, green hills, mountains, rivers, streams, cows, sheep, condors, ravens, eagles, hawks. Frisco is a speedy experience, I accidentally swallowed all the little speed balls instead of a quarter like I'd planned after already having a whole one in my system from the drive. I buzzed through the electric green and red-lit night, high as a kite and drinking whiskey and beer like a maniac. The show goes off without a hitch and the crowd loves us, not a bad start. The hall we're playing in is old and magnificent, a vaudeville theater from the days of yore.

After the show I start talking with the lead singer of another band on the bill with us, a very tall, skinny, dark-haired siren. She talks in hushed tones full of murky innuendoes and barely concealable nocturnal desires. She has a cabalistic ring hanging on a chain around her neck. Her name is Magdalena, she's a California native, and a good foot taller than me in her high heels. I don't care about her height, want to climb her like a redwood and see what's under her hood, but just then Kiarash walks in and Magdalena's gaze tells me she'd rather let him lay her down beside the sea of lust at dawn, so I quickly introduce them and leave to walk the streets.

How many times have I been to San Francisco? How many times have I been here with dreams packed in my bags and said, 'This is it!' Four? Five? I think this is the sixth time I've played old San Fran with its mystical fog, crazed sun, green hills, and that end-of-the-line finality calling out to the rest of the world.

I walk outside and wander the streets surrounding the venue. Around a dark alley a bum, who turns out to be a poet, starts a conversation with me, wants to sell me his poetry.

'I only have a few coins on me, is that enough?' I say.

'Naw, man, I'm selling these for three bucks a piece,' he says.

'Do you sell many of 'em?'

'Eh, sometimes, not really. You know, most people aren't really into poetry anymore.'

'Yeah. I wish I had a little more money. I'd sure buy one and see what your stuff's like, man. I gotta cigarette though if you want.'

He takes a smoke from me and we say goodbye in the dream-filled night. I walk the streets and wonder what will become of this tour. We must go down this road to get to the next one. How many roads, Lord? Then a voice inside my head: *You had found the right road long ago and have come to it again and again but keep choosing to take another each and every time. You will have a choice once more at the end of this one. The end of this road will lead you right back to the one you found long ago. Will you choose to take it?*

Next day we play in LA. The show is fantastic, the crowd is with us the whole way. The screams after each song are piercing. They're in love with us. After the show we get invited to a beachfront house in Malibu. I can't tell if the gorgeous model prancing about is with the guy who owns the house or not, but I'm doing my best to lay the groundwork for an eventual full-frontal assault. She is beautiful and young, of the gapped-tooth variety and dumber than dirt. Her taste in music is laughable, her knowledge of art almost nil, but I'm giving her the benefit of the doubt. She looks like a young Mariel Hemingway. Every test proves in my favor, she follows me outside to smoke whenever I go, offers to show me around the grounds, walks down to the beach with me. We smoke a joint and talk and talk and talk. I am a sucker like the rest, am laying it on thick and ahead on points, have to make a move. She's not with the guy who owns the house, but engaged to her high-school sweetheart from her hometown somewhere in the Sierra Nevada, and so the conversation comes to an abrupt end. She seems suddenly offended and leaves, her blue eyes no longer glowing with delight.

The hour is late and everyone else seems to be sleeping in the big house. I stay down there and stare out onto the undulating current. Time warps in front of this relativistic observer and taunts with her siren charms. The billows beckon while the North Star blinks and the Santa Ana winds become katabatic above me.

And so I stood there in front of that dark ocean with its waves crashing, yelling, 'Come on, you big bad sea, you talked to Jack Kerouac, now talk to me!' *And the ocean started talking and I was all ears, knelt on the wet sand with arms outstretched breathing deeply that salty ocean air and humming to the tunes the sea was singing. It sang so loudly my ears bled invisible lead molecules and I heard voices screeching and foam was spraying into my face. I was drunk and stoned on the sea's mystical powers. Come on, you big bad ocean of lust and awe, you god, you monster, you unthinkably mad thing with all those ships and seamen you've swallowed that now belong to you, with all the secrets of humanity digesting forever in your entrancing waters, come on and sing to me! I am yours now. Take me while the rest of the world sleeps soundly up on the hill. Take me in secret while my friends slumber on their optimistic beds. Carry me pole-ward and equatorial in the same breath then drag me across the seamount chains. Tell me about your old Panthalassa self for I want to be Polynesia-bound. Show me your xenoliths from Tuamotu to Melanesia, from Fiji to New Caledonia, and at last Terra Australis for this is a new age of discovery!* And suddenly I realized I was neck-deep in the abyss of the Pacific and a dark wave crashed on top of me and I tumbled around like a piece of driftwood, scraped the bottom, and floated up again.

Sober, I swam back to shore, where I dragged myself across the sand and laid on my back to stare at the stars in wonder and waited for the light of day to come and dry my insides out.

We take off for Houston the next day. Goodbye, blessed California, heaven on Earth, land of plenty. When I'll be back I do not know. Until next time, dear heavenly blest soil protected by saints and angels, a thousand kisses, all of my love. Into Arizona now, desert landscapes, xerophytes, ghosts of the Sobaipuri calling to me, the Pima calling, the Colorado calling, Grand Canyon calling, but we can't stop and must keep driving. Then the land of enchantment, Nuevo Mexico, the Pueblo people calling, Mesa Verde, my Navajo brothers calling, my Apache friends calling, Saint Francis of Assisi, Coronado still looking for his seven golden cities. One day I will lie in the white sands but not today. We must keep moving.

The Lone Star State is calling, the passage awaits and we cross the Franklin Mountains and drive through El Paso at nightfall. We play a show in Houston, the band and I growing more and more distant each moment, our thoughts and emotions no longer running parallel. I am changing fast, morphing. The next stage awaits. Rebirth waits patiently but not until the rituals are complete. I will not be drinking mead from a human skull just yet, no white robes just yet but soon. I'm closer to the mysteries, closer to the secrets. I can feel it.

Now our caravan is in New Orleans. Each visit to this orphic city has come at a transitional time for me. I've been a whore and a saint, now I find it hard to walk down the streets, must keep my carnal desires at bay, and it's easy since I'm broke. I don't want to go any farther, want to bid my friends a fond farewell and go back to Texas, to my family. I need a fresh start.

Then we're off to Hot Springs, Arkansas, with its natural thermal water flowing from deep beneath the earth and its magical quartz crystals sending pure mystical energy into our souls. Here I have a momentary lapse and fall for a singer of a female duo playing on the same bill as us. The one who entrances me is a wild vamp from Nashville, another young girl, a Cherokee, Choctaw, Mohawk, with problems, and totally the wrong kind of woman for me. I watch her every move from the second row, she stares into my eyes and holds her gaze. I stare right back and for a full twenty seconds she's just singing to me. The other girl in the act seems to be totally spellbound by the one I like too. After the show I go up to the two of them and say, 'Good show,' and all that stuff, ask her name.

'Priscilla,' she says in a heavy southern drawl. We talk for a long time sitting on the floor of the green room and sing along to Waylon Jennings songs she's playing on her iPhone. She's surprised an Iranian dude knows country songs. I tell her I'm also a Texan and love country music. 'Old country, of course.'

Then her lesbian admirer bandmate, who also acts as their manager and had gone to get the money, comes over and takes her away to the next town on their itinerary. The two of them together remind me of Drusilla and Bernice, the wicked daughters of King Herod, but hell I ain't Paul and this ain't the judgment hall at Caesarea. I do have a feeling though that soon someone will accuse me of sedition, and rightly so for I am sowing the seeds of rebellion. I don't even ask for Priscilla's number before she's taken away. I figure if anything is in the cards for us, it'll happen by chance on a hot Corinthian eve by a river, in the dark, with the crickets chirping outside the tent.

'You must be an Aquarius,' I told this other girl after Priscilla left.

'Yes I am, wow. How did you know?' she said.

'I can just tell. Tell me more about what you did on that organic farm you were talking about, will ya?'

She began to tell me about it, told me how they worked together and dined together under starry skies, momentarily taking me away to distant magic landscapes and designs of my own mind. When she first spoke to me I was sitting with Kiarash. Both of us silent as monks.

'What are you doing? Plotting?' she said out of nowhere. That happened to be precisely what I was doing at the time, plotting my next move. Her intuitive question pregnant with certain knowledge led me to correctly guess her zodiac sign. I was not yet able to diagrammatically triangulate my problems but I was getting closer to doing so. I was as always not yet fully aware of being only temporarily of the earth. My reasoning was not yet vibrating correctly. I was not cosmically attuned.

# Last Night

Last night of the tour now and once again another half-assed attempt, by me, at getting laid for the sake of nothing, and nothing coming of it, and thank God for that. Another Midwestern midwife but this time it's a no go. After a while it's apparent she doesn't like the vibrations emanating from my soul. Why these midwives on every tour? Must have a metaphysical meaning, no? Is it a foreshadowing of rebirth? To be born again is not a purely evangelical Christian concept. The Druids and Eleusinians believed in it, as did those belonging to the cult of Mithras and many others.

From Chicago to New York our little caravan is in tatters. A change is coming and in the blink of an eye we're back in Brooklyn. The stage is set for an upheaval. It's okay, for all things must pass and life is for learning.

# The End

'We should go out tonight, just me and you. I know just the place. We'll find something for sure,' Kiarash says to me before leaving for work in the morning. He goes out almost every night while I stay home to drink and write. He thinks a night out on the town will be good for me. I'm not in the band anymore. It just didn't work out.

'Come on, it'll be open bar,' Kiarash says.

'I hate open bars though.'

'Just come out and talk to some girls. You and me make a great team, remember? Let's get out there again, come on. Dari is working the door at Cameo and Siamak is bartending at Ding Dong, and Matt is DJ-ing at Electric Room. We'll get in for free and have some free drinks. Aren't you sick of sitting at home?'

'I'll think about it,' I say.

'All right, good. I'll see you later.'

I sit in the kitchen, light a cigarette, and chew on the thought of stepping out into the savage night with him. The New York germ-plasm night, the ovarian night full of wild shouts and sulfurous intimations, the incandescent phallic night, one night after another, one long night, night of nights. Me with my dulcimer and Kiarash with his lyre, skidding along the oily streets, eyes twinkling with that midnight sheen, gizzards bursting, pineal-gland pretension overload, dust off the old suede shoes and step to the street beat, down, down, down to the underground. Down to the streets alive with decay to see what's there that you might have missed. Circular motion dizziness mixed with vitality overload, sex overdrive, masculine overhaul. Not a hair out of place and joining the race with no rest, 'cause it's a test. I'm all in for the bet 'cause I'm the best!

You can't fret until it's time to quit and there ain't no quitting tonight, Jack, or tomorrow, not in this town, never was and never will be. This ain't like the rest of America, buster. Fall in or get out. Hell is where you thought it was, right here! Let's see how good you smile, we count teeth in this city. Hike up your skirt and let's see how good you squirt. Piss down my lungs, I'm a nasty motherfucker, didn't you know? Hang on to your girl lest you lose her to another pest. Everybody is a sucker. You think you can still make it dressed in black? Hear ye, hear ye, my ass in a chimney, go catch a pole in your hole. Sit on it, twerp! Climb the towers of power or slide down a sewer in your best suit, master blaster. Open up and say 'ah,' give me all your money or I'll take it all from you, your call.

I've walked the endless plank and don't have the heart or stomach for it anymore, too many gleaming guns in the night and the scent of fear emanating from my enigmatic innards, black smoke funneling out of my ears and racing downward through the parting pavement. The cold blue light of day will come and wash over my chilled bones then the winds will blow dust in my fiery eyes. The fire will turn to ash then the ash will be in my eyes, blinding me, see? And none of it amounts to a hill of beans in Juarez. I'll be blonded by a brunette and shaking my ass for a crowd of insatiable hyenas in three-piece business suits, rubbing my engorged center on their enlarged ones, have to fondle their pricks for a tip of the hat, my whorish gills sucking, breathing metaphors and swallowing matadors.

Barometric pressure rising over the coastal inlets, Kill Van Kull exploding with lava and oozing cosmic ether from the crevices. I'm clutching the torch and holding it high above to light the bay for the ghost ships. Lighting a match under the Fourth of July fireworks to set off the synchronized agony of dawn while motorized fizz puppies shitting on streets and pissing up skyscrapers stop momentarily to realize that nobody's there to clean it up. Every ship and tugboat in the bay is blowing horns in discordant unison for no reason at all. There's no business like show business and no fuck like a royal fuck. Devour me, cartilage and all. You look hungry and mean but I'm a good

Samaritan and a good sport. Paint me murderous pink and parade me down 5th Circle of Hell Avenue, I'm feeling sassy tonight! Play me like a doom harp for all to hear, deflower my feminine half and detonate the masculine one. Grind me down to interplanetary dust, and lift my curse.

Now twilight is quivering and ever so timidly approaching. The filth will be washed away on the correct street-cleaning day and not a minute sooner. The filth will just have to bake in the hot sun until then. Birds will swoop down from the smog clouds for crumbs of shit and rats will jump towards the indigo sky for they dream of flight like the rest of us. Infinity dreams about finite finality. Hurry before the sale ends! Masticating mutable mobsters of monster-mania-land stand at attention before the new czars of industry while moles of mumbo-jumbo-land predict the bright future to come. Mules of Meal City sing lost hymns of Atlantis while the chaste cheaters of Holywood are all out in tiny dresses to get a piece, after giving one of course.

New York City, Singles City, Fuck City, Suck City, how can anyone be lonely here, by God! Musical chairs played with dynamite strapped to the last chair so the winner can also be the loser too. It's a fair new world after all and the brave will get their asses handed to them just like everybody else. I think I'll join the masses of advancing and retreating cunts and cocks on parade, why not? I'll fall in with the crowd and see where the mob takes me. We'll march on down to the middle of the marshes and take turns drowning each other in shallow water until there's no one left then walk back home. On second thoughts I'll just stay here and rearrange my brain tonight.

Then a voice in my head saying: why don't you throw out those alcoholic, drug-addicted thought processes and step to the real street beat? The one that teaches you to take the good with the bad, the one that makes you see things for what they are. You can't be clear with an unclean soul. It doesn't matter what city streets you are walking down, old Alexandria, Damascus, Rome, San Francisco, you have to fix yourself.

In her bathing suit with just a loose shirt Allison walks around the house she shares with two males and a female but there's nothing I can say to her now because she isn't mine any longer.

'You're so touchy feely,' she said, and, 'It was a rebound, he was nice to me.'

'Well, I'm glad he was nice at least and not an asshole,' I told her.

She's been touched and loved by another and it makes me nauseous but what can I do? When she disrobes I have to look away, though I manage to sneak a peek anyway. Everything is wrong but exactly the way it has to be. Surreal the way things have worked out.

The bus dropped me off at a gas station, I dragged my suitcase into the bathroom and washed my face and brushed my teeth. She drove up in her new car, got out with tears in her eyes, and we held each other tightly for a minute. 'Get in,' she said, and we drove along silently. Later on there was the hotel, no sex, she was on her period, just pushing and pulling. We played on the beach and collected seashells. I'm sitting at the Greyhound bus station waiting to go back to New York. On the TV the protesters in Turkey are supposedly growing in number on the square and some woman is attempting to swim a hundred miles up the Atlantic coast without a shark cage. Allison was crying after saying goodbye to me outside of the station. I didn't turn around and tried not to cry. You don't want to be a crying man walking into the bus station, somebody might eat you alive like that man who approached me looking at my suitcase saying, 'This is my hustle.' I gave him the I'm-from-New-York look and walked on. Wild fires burning in Colorado, smoke rising into space, nothing Allison and I can do about that. Pulling out of Jacksonville now and asking it to keep my baby safe, up to Savannah then Fayetteville. Goodbye, palm trees.

'I think you can see how much healthier she looks now. That was the road to destruction she was on,' her mother had said in her long flowing summer dress while Allison was holding her niece, spinning her around, and making her laugh. Allison was thunderous at nights, saying things like, 'If I were you I would back off because I'm not putting up with shit like that anymore, from you or anybody else.'

We drove to Saint Augustine and went to this amazing seafood place.

'Honey, this is the south, we put bacon in everything,' the old jovial waitress informed Allison.

'Oh, I know. I was just checking,' Allison told her with a smile. So we ordered the pickled beets with our fish instead of the string beans. At the breakfast place this morning they had a sign that read 'One day at the beach is worth a month in town.' And Allison said, 'You betcha.' The bus is passing Cumberland Island national seashore and don't you know you've got to turn your lights on when it's raining? Thanking old Eisenhower for making this here Interstate system possible while we drive over Crooked River, which really is pretty damn crooked, looks like the Mississippi viewed from an airplane. Allison loves boiled peanuts, eats them while lounging on her bed.

'I've had to rebuild my life,' she said with her blue eyes sparkling. 'Will you come down and get me sometime?' her blue eyes a bit wet now.

Cathead Creek just ahead, storks and herons flying about. Who are all these people on this bus? There are workers giving the Savannah bus station a major facelift for the shiny future, the passengers are eating chips and candy from the vending machines. We go over a bridge, the city becomes more industrial, grain elevators, port of Savannah with its giant cranes to the left, in front, open marshland. The whole house smelled of dirty dog, her roommate's; Allison's room smelled of incense and perfume. She had a fresh coat of paint on the walls, also her Van Gogh reproduction and a few other lovely pictures tacked up. A vintage lamp of the French opium-den variety threw a soft sensuous light around the small room.

*Tremulous mortifications circulating melodiously, intervening without jesting, serenading the serene side of me, taking me to the shores of distance with unrelenting patience, dazzling my bottom heart past drowned soul as I awaken from another savage dream on the bus.* Two middle-aged men talk of their roofing business behind me as a lone passenger snores away to my left. The bus rolls on down the highway, the sun is going down, and the landscape is at once majestic and chilling. I am an evacuee with a steel-gray aura fawning. Analyzing the same old haunting abstractions camouflaged by absolute beliefs.

A billboard reads Fireworks Ahead, another reads Full Auto Machine Guns, Georgia Peaches. There's an old plantation house next to a high-school football field. An old man and an old woman are hitchhiking by the side of the road. Allison and I walked through the antique shop across the way from the seafood restaurant and once again glided on misty golden-hued daydreams of a future together. Later we fell into a delicious effervescent sleep, side by side in the humid Floridian night, walking in between one another's dreams while the world went on turning. She was no longer mine, had experienced magical spirit-scorching visions on the foothills leading to the Caribbean lowlands. Allison, woman of the sea, traveling island girl, healing soul, savior of lost children, my love, my one and only. I'm leaving you now and see that you have already left me. Let me tell you of one of the aphoristic statements of Pythagoras, which reads: *Having departed from your house, turn not back; for the furies will be your attendants.* So turn not back, sweet lady, lest you turn into a pillar of salt, and I won't either. Forward, only forward, and may you find happiness.

'I'm just starting to see it now, you know, something that I know you've known for a while, that it all has to happen this way, all the madness and the technology overload, the wars and deaths and market crashes, all of it, all the mistakes and more. All we can really do is go with it and learn as individuals and as a whole.' I wasn't a hundred per cent convinced but was talking as if I were, sitting there in my black jeans still unwashed from the bus rides to and from Florida, with a white T-shirt last worn by and smelling of Allison's sweet perfume, a denim blue dead-stock vest from the fifties purchased at her friend's shop by the St. John's river, a beaded Shawnee necklace around my neck, brown boots on my feet, unshaven and smoking a cigarette while talking to Manuchehr. The rest of the kids were at some party.

'I know what you mean,' Manuchehr began in his quiet respectful manner, sitting cross-legged and smoking his rolled tobacco. 'I learned that in Iran. It seemed like whenever we pushed to get out it didn't somehow work. Only when we finally let go and went with the flow.'

These guys have done really well for themselves after all, I thought. Their stories of travel around Iran, India, and Turkey are incredible and numerous. Now they are in America and continuing to go with the flow.

I was meaning to also say to him that by the same token there has to be people like me questioning things and I know that on one level all my problems and roaming and ramblings can be boiled down to addiction and financial trouble or not skipping and hopping to the current world beat, immigration, and war, but damn it I burn and yearn like all the others burned and yearned. Is it all over and done with? Have we moved on or were 'we' always past it? I have to be what I am. I know I've been here before and written things down on papyrus and parchment, wax and vellum. On wood, terracotta, and tablets of stone. I know I've searched the lost libraries of Baghdad and Alexandria, know that I've asked questions of weary people wandering the lost harbors of time, studied a hundred lifetimes under the tutelage of great masters, why then can't I remember a single word of it all? Alas I am a modern man, a stupid man sleepy and tired, having to resort to finding meaningless jobs in meaningless cities. Hey, cool it, buster! Is it meaningless to pay your rent? Maybe, but you better pay it lest you get kicked out into the dirty mean lonely streets of humanity where nobody gives a hoot in cold dark hell whether you live or perish beneath feet. Take any meaningless job you can and thank the morning star. Beg for it, you idiot. They are shooting rich folks into space, planting chips in brains, making artificial limbs, and here you are talking a whole lot of baloney about ancient dust clouds. Get up and march to the street beat before they press a button and vanish your sorry ass, before they think you obsolete.

Look into your amorphous soul and try to arrange the bright crepuscular rays into parallel bands. Take the ripple clouds of your delicate white filament thoughts and hope for a naked singularity. Take your ephemeral nature and mold it into something manageable. Find the prime meridian of your mind. Remember all of the times traveling in cars and buses when you stared up into the zodiacal light with face pressed against the window wondering if it was Neptune up there and making up your own theories of terrestrial dynamical time? Remember how all thought fizzed away from your mind to circle the galactic corona a while? Remember how you begged Venus to come closer and unveil herself? The Lagoon Nebula used to call unto you. Hydra, Corvus, Antilia, Alpha Virginis, and the watery constellations would tell you that linear time was divisible. You are of the earth and the divine is within you like it is within everybody else. So don't be afraid, forgive yourself, and stay crazy. The light is not at the end of the tunnel but everywhere and waiting.

# Afterword

*August 2012*

I will never forget my first impression of Ali.

My wife Manuela and I hosted – with the help of some friends in New York – an exhibition called 'Made in Iran' in downtown Manhattan, with the Iranian brothers Icy & Sot, two street artists who had just made the transition from Tabriz, their hometown in Iran, to New York. This was the city they had been dreaming of, where they would meet their friends: musicians, artists, and skaters who had already left their country behind them, realizing that the impossibility of returning to Iran would be the price they'd have to pay for the freedom to express themselves – in art.

Manuela and I had already been working with the brothers for some years, staging their first solo show outside Iran, in Amsterdam in 2011. Ali was preparing for a performance in the back of the gallery; he would play first, followed by a short gig by the Yellow Dogs.

He was dressed in black, tuning his acoustic guitar,

looking quite intense and pumped up. When he started playing, I watched the manager of all the 'kids' (Ali's loving way of describing his friends in the novel, which I was not aware of at that moment), who was also named Ali: Ali Salehezadeh. He mouthed: 'Great musician. Not an easy guy.'

Needless to say, I liked him immediately. He played a couple of very emotional and powerful songs, and I liked those too.

Usually I am not that into singer-songwriters; I prefer relentless noise and walls of sound. Singer-songwriters – come on, what's new since good old Bob?

Ali.

He was the real deal.

I complimented him afterwards, when he and the Yellow Dogs and Icy & Sot were smoking in the back garden.

Back in my hotel later that evening, I googled him and stumbled upon a great performance from years before on YouTube, which resonated with the same intense, powerful, and mesmerizing feeling I had experienced in the gallery – Ali with his guitar, looking a bit like Prince, stamping his feet to accompany himself to the music.

Yeah, I thought, this guy is good.

*September 2012*
Two weeks later I got married – for a third and last time – to Manuela, and not long after that I received an email from Ali.

> Dear Oscar,
>
> I hope this email finds you well. We met at Icy & Sot's opening in New York where I played a small set of music.
>
> I have been working on a novel which is now finished, and after talking to Icy & Sot about them perhaps doing some cover art for it was told about your publishing house. I looked on the website and was immediately impressed by the roster of authors. Hunter S. Thompson is one of my absolute heroes and to see his face on the top corner sent a

shock of excitement through my hungover body.

I have not tried my hand at any publishers, editors, or agents in the States as of yet, but will of course try those traditional routes at some point. My idea is to self-publish the thing no matter what happens. The novel is called *American Immigrant* and is about someone like myself: immigrant, war child, rock 'n' roller, artist trying to live in a modern world he finds infuriating/exhilarating. There is an insurgent political bent to the writing, also lots of sex, drugs, and rock 'n' roll. There are characters very similar to the Yellow Dogs, as well. I lived with the Dogs for almost two years and we got to have some fun. I think it could be the great Iranian-American novel, or at least that's what I'll call it until someone proves me wrong.

I was wondering if it would be possible for me to send you a manuscript or portions of the book for some feedback.

I realize this might be asking a lot but since this is my first foray into the publishing world I figure I can be a little reckless and attribute it to my inexperience.

I look forward to your response and thank you for your time.

Best wishes,
Ali Eskandarian

The manuscript landed on my desk another two weeks later. Reading the first two words – *American Immigrant* – on the stack of paper I thought, My God, I truly hope the book is better than the title.

I waited some time before I started reading. I was in two minds: was this like saving up the last bite from a delicious plate of food, or, quite the opposite, opening that envelope from your taxman?

I was afraid to be disappointed, obviously.

Then I started reading, and I could not believe how good the novel was – fresh, funny, wild, uncensored, eloquent, raw, uncut. This guy really was the real deal. How the hell had he managed to pull this off all by himself, without any editorial guidance or advice?

I wrote to him: 'I will publish this baby, no matter what.'

I also wanted to know more about him. This is how Ali replied:

> My family and I moved out of Iran in '89 and went to Germany, then moved to the US (Dallas, TX) in '92. I studied theater and later film production in college, worked in film production until very recently to pay the bills, and played music. I moved to New York in 2003, played music as a solo artist and eventually got a record deal in 2006 with Wildflower Records, which is owned by the folk artist Judy Collins. During those years and up to

> 2009, I was pretty busy with numerous shows and tours, played all the festivals and opened up for among other people Peter Murphy of Bauhaus (North American Tour) and Judy Collins (small tour of England). I was also a part of the Freedom Glory Project (collaboration of Iranian artists against the regime) during the Iranian Elections of 2008. I eventually got myself out of the record contract. Since 2010 I've been involved with the Yellow Dogs as friends and collaborators on shows and music. I've also made a short film and done documentary work. The manuscript I sent you is my first book but I've been writing or trying to write for many years and hope to write as much as I can.

'There is just one problem,' I wrote to Ali. 'I am a Dutch publisher. I'll need an English/American editor to get the book into perfect shape and then we can publish it – to maximum effect.

'Oh, and another thing. Let's change the title, to *Golden Years*.'

Ali wrote back: 'I like this title a lot, it of course also conjures up the Bowie/rock 'n' roll thing, which is great. And it looks good in print as well.'

I don't like waiting. I set up a Facebook page for Ali, a Twitter account, and a page on Medium.com, which we use at Lebowski in order to publish stories, poems, and all kinds of texts of note, and we just got started.

*October 2012*

We began serializing the novel on Medium.com in October, for I thought it would be a great way to draw attention to the book – from international publishers, editors, fans – and to get it out there on Facebook and Twitter.

We emailed from time to time. I had asked Vicki Satlow, a literary agent in Milan, to represent him; we made plans for him to come over to the London or Frankfurt Book Fairs, where we could introduce him to all our friends in the publishing world. We were sure everybody would be impressed by both him and his novel.

In the meantime, we kept on publishing excerpts from the novel, and Ali wrote that he was thinking of maybe moving to Germany for some months so he could be closer. It would make it easier getting him hooked up with the right people.

A year passed . . .

*November 2013*

On 10 November 2013 I wrote to Ali saying that I had just uploaded another excerpt from the novel. In the evening, hours before disaster struck, he answered, saying that he loved the image I had chosen for it.

The next day Manuela and I got a phone call from Kimberley in Los Angeles, one of the friends who had helped us big time when we hosted the exhibition with

Icy & Sot. Ali Akbar Rafie, a former member of another New York-based group, the Free Keys, who had been kicked out of the band some months before, had gone to the house where all the 'kids' lived with just one thing on his mind: havoc.

He shot and killed Ali Eskandarian. He shot and killed Arash and Soroush 'Looloosh' Farazmand, the two brothers who played in the Yellow Dogs. He shot and wounded Sot (Icy remained unharmed), before killing himself.

*November 2015*

The book you are holding in your hands, dear reader, has come to light thanks to some amazing people. First of all, Ali's parents, Mahmood and Nadia, his brother Sam, and his sister Baharak. I am very thankful that they trusted me to handle Ali's literary legacy, leaving me with an orphaned manuscript that needed a home.

And homes we found, Vicki Satlow and I. Lee Brackstone, publisher at Faber Social in the UK, fell in love with the novel, just like we did. We see this publishing venture as a *ménage à trois*. Lee has been instrumental in getting this 'baby' published: not only did he do a fabulous editorial job, he also promoted the book to all his friends – and there are many – in the literary world.

A word of thanks also to Ali, Icy, Sot, Obash, and Koory. We are one family.

*Golden Years* will be published in the UK, US, Spain, Portugal, Romania, Germany, Holland, and Belgium. We hope many other countries will follow.

Let's keep on calling *Golden Years* Ali's Great Iranian-American Novel, until someone proves him wrong.

Oscar van Gelderen